Black Woods

Also by T. K. Fairclough

The Golden Idol: A Rick and Hugo Adventure

Black Woods

Another Rick and Hugo Adventure

T. K. Fairclough

Copyright © 2021 T. K. Fairclough

All rights reserved, including the right to reproduce this book, or portions thereof in any form. No part of this text may be reproduced, transmitted, downloaded, decompiled, reverse engineered, or stored, in any form or introduced into any information storage and retrieval system, in any form or by any means, whether electronic or mechanical without the express written permission of the author.

Black Woods is a work of fiction. All of the names, characters, organisations and events portrayed in this novel are either products of the author's fevered imagination or are used fictitiously.

ISBN: 9798595358286

For Jobo

Acknowledgements

I would like to say a big thank you to the following people for the help, support and encouragement they gave me while writing this book and afterwards: Malcolm Dervan, Anna Maria Rengo, Belinda Bennett, Helen Munden, Arthur Brett, John Fennessey Kennedy, the staff of Greggs at the Beaumont Leys Shopping Centre for their good humour, excellent customer service and products and the staff at the Beaumont Leys Library for their technical assistance.

I would also like to give a special mention to Malcolm Dervan for permission to use his song 'Sittin' in me pants at Christmas' and to Lyn Scates for permission to use her poem 'The Train Spotter'.

Chapter One

D'ya ever wish sometimes you should've kept your big mouth shut? Me too! I knew as soon as I said to Hugo let's visit Gotham, that I had said the wrong thing, from the devilish look in his eye. Whenever I had been waiting for the 154 bus to take me back from Loughborough to Beaufort, there was always the South Notts Number 1 double-decker bus to Nottingham parked up. Along the side of the bus below the windows it read Loughborough>East Leake>Gotham>Clifton>Nottingham and I always fancied going to Gotham because of it sounding like Gotham City of Batman fame and because of that fame the village sign has been stolen a few times.

We'd planned to go to Gotham on Saturday and left Beaufort early this morning on the 154 bus to Loughborough and visited the Devonshire Fisheries Takeaway and Restaurant for a cooked breakfast, and then had a look around the market and charity shops before making our way to Stand BA at the bus station.

I should've cottoned on something was afoot, when Hugo had brought his big rucksack with him and said he had to nip to the toilet, and now as we were waiting to board the bus to Gotham, he had changed his clothing and was sat next to me dressed from head to foot as Batman; not as Adam West's Caped Crusader but as Christian Bale's black clad Dark Knight! I just hoped there wasn't a village called Metropolis within bus distance from Beaufort!

"Two returns to Gotham please," Hugo said, mimicking the gruff voice of the Batman from *The LEGO Batman Movie*, as we boarded the bus.

"No Batmobile today?" The driver replied straight faced.

"No, the voice activated weapons system is playing up plus it's due for its MOT," Hugo retorted, equally straight faced.

"Oh right," the driver replied with a laugh.

"Can you give us a shout when we get to Gotham please?"

"Yeah," the driver replied looking agog as we found some seats at the back of the bus, with Hugo drawing strange looks and titters from the other passengers.

The bus left at 13:33 and wound its way out of Loughborough and Leicestershire and on into Nottinghamshire, passing the mediaeval Church of St John the Baptist on the left and then on past Stanford on Soar and turned right into Leake Lane, stopping along the route to let off passengers and take on some who all looked at Hugo and gave a chuckle or sniggered while finding a seat downstairs or going upstairs.

"I was in Poundland the other day getting some black socks, and as I queued up, I overheard this old guy telling two women that he used to be in Showaddwaddy!"

"What did he look like, Bert?"

"I reckon he must have been in his late sixties, early seventies and had long silvery-white hair, with long black sideburns and a horseshoe moustache, oh…and he had a walking stick."

"Did you recognise him?"

"No, but he definitely wasn't the frontman, Dave Bartram."

"They were from Leicester, so stands a good chance, one or more of them live locally, Bert."

"Yeah, you're right, Hugo."

Turning right the bus travelled a short distance along the A6006, and then turned left onto Loughborough Road at the end of which the driver turned left into East Leake which was in Nottinghamshire but had a Leicestershire postcode. The bus drove along Main Street, passing The Bulls Head on the left and a row of shops on either side, where more passengers got off and on and would have a laugh or a giggle on spotting Hugo, who just sat there and lapped up all the attention and even posed when a few of the passengers were bold enough to point their mobile phones at him and take a photo.

"D'ya know anything about Gotham, Hugo?"

"Only that it's where Batman lives."

"I meant where we're headed now, not Gotham City."

"No, Bert."

"So you've never heard of 'The Wise Men of Gotham'?"

2

"Err no!"

"Okay, well in 1200, King John was on his way to Nottingham, and his route would take him through the village of Gotham. Now, under an ancient law, wherever the king travelled, the route then became a public highway and the locals would be financially responsible for its construction and maintenance. Well, 'The Wise Men of Gotham' as the story goes, got wind of this and they hatched a plan to feign madness by carrying out irrational tasks around the village to avoid the highway being constructed.

The ruse worked, as the King's messengers reported on the mad behaviour of the locals back to him and the highway was re-routed around Gotham, as in those days madness was thought to be infectious."

"What kind of irrational tasks?"

"I think there was one where they were observed trying to drown an eel in pool of water."

"Very strange, Bert."

"Yeah," I replied laughing.

"The American writer Washington Irving who wrote *Rip Van Winkle* and *The Legend of Sleepy Hollow*, also created under a pseudonym the short lived satirical periodical *Salmagundi*, which lampooned New York culture and politics and nicknamed the city Gotham after the village of Gotham in Nottinghamshire, whose inhabitants pretended to be mad. Then in 1939, writer Milton 'Bill' Finger and artist Robert 'Bob' Kane created the Batman character for DC Comics and Finger is credited with coming up with the name Gotham City after finding the firm of Gotham Jewelers in the New York City phone directory."

"How do you know all this?"

"I looked it up on the internet, when I was in the library yesterday."

"Very interesting, Bert."

The bus left East Leake on the Gotham Road passing the village fire station and then further on it passed the British Gypsum UK Service Centre and Rushcliffe Halt, a heritage railway station of the Great Central Railway.

"There's a village called Bunny off to the right, Bert," Hugo said sniggering like Muttley. I looked to where he was pointing and there was indeed a sign saying 'Bunny 3 miles' along Bunny Lane.

The bus then cruised past Rushcliffe Golf Club along the long and straight Leake Road, cutting through the Nottinghamshire countryside with fields of cattle and sheep on both sides, while stopping intermittently to drop off and take on passengers.

"There's the famous Gotham sign, Bert," Hugo excitedly cried, pointing to the left.

"Can't be far now," I replied.

"I hope not," replied Hugo, removing something from one of the pouches on his utility belt. "I was hoping to stick this on the Gotham sign and get you to take a photo of me posing beside it," Hugo said handing me a sticker which was a black silhouette of a bat. "Where did you get this from?"

"Inside *The Dark Knight Manual* I bought from the Age UK bookshop in Loughborough a few months ago, in the centre of the book was a whole bunch of stickers."

"It looks a fair old distance back to the sign from the village."

"Hmm," uttered Hugo sounding a tad disappointed.

"Got a joke for you, what's yellow and smells like green paint?"

"Don't know," Hugo said after pondering for a while.

"Yellow paint!" I answered.

"Good one, Bert," Hugo replied with a grin.

The bus passed the Nottingham City Transport garage on the left and after a minute or two the driver shouted "Gotham," as the bus stopped just after the Cuckoo Bush Inn.

"How often are the buses back?" Hugo asked the driver.

"Every twenty minutes from the stop opposite," the driver stated.

"Thank you," Hugo said as we got off the bus and I'm sure I heard somebody from the bus shout after us 'dinna, dinna, dinna, dinna!' Hugo waved to the passengers who were looking at him through the bus windows as the driver pulled away.

I looked at my mobile phone it was 14:02, up ahead of us was a white single storey building with a sign on the end facing us saying 'Gotham News' which was the local newsagents, convenience store, off-licence and post office. We turned around and headed in the opposite direction towards the hexagonal shaped structure surrounded by metal railings. "Take a photo of me, Bert," Hugo said handing me his mobile phone as we came across an old fingerpost that read East Leake 3, Loughborough 7 pointing to my left and Clifton 3½, Nottingham 6½ pointing to my right. Hugo posed beside it as I took some photos of him.

We bimbled along into The Square and came to the hexagonal structure, which was a Grade II listed building known as the 'Well House' which was built in 1862 to house the cistern, with the water being pumped from a local spring. The villagers had to wait until 1933 before they were connected to the mains water supply in Nottingham, which lay seven miles north-northeast of the village.

The inside of the pointed roof was circular and divided into six wooden segments like a pizza, five of which chronicled the history of Gotham from 1086 when it is mentioned in the *Domesday Book* to 2016. Around the base of the structure were two benches where locals and visitors could sit, talk and read the information panels, together with several cardboard boxes of books arranged around a central stone block. "What's with the books, Bert?"

"I'm not a hundred percent sure, but when I lived in a high-rise block of flats, in the foyer was a table and anything the residents didn't want any longer they would place on the table and the other residents were free to take whatever they wanted, it saved throwing them out I suppose, these books are maybe summat like that."

"Hmm, Hugo mumbled.

We walked on between The Sun Inn on the left and the twelfth-century Church of St Lawrence on the right and at the end of The Square turned left and came across The Gotham Arms.

The red brick Victorian pub had white framed, grid pattern windows and a slate roof with three evenly spaced tall chimneys. It did not have a traditional hanging pub sign, but above the main entrance was a large horizontal rectangle of black painted wood with The Gotham Arms painted in white and then the date 1852.

"This will do, Bert!" Hugo cried as we entered the pub through the open grey door which had wooden boxes sprouting red and white flowers sat either side and on the left was a sandwich board that stated they were taking Festive bookings now.

The hubbub of chatter died in the patron's throats as they all turned around to look at us. It was like a scene from one of those old Hammer horror movies where strangers entered a village inn nestling in the shadow of the Carpathian Mountains in Transylvania, seeking a meal and a drink after a long coach journey, and the frightened locals fall deathly silent and eye them with suspicion.

The bar was full of predominantly middle-aged to older gentlemen, with some tittering and giggling, a good few rolled their eyes, while others sat wide eyed catching flies and the remainder just looked astounded!

"Hasn't anybody seen Batman in Gotham before?" Hugo said, breaking the frigid silence.

"It's pronounced Goat-em," remarked a balding, thick set man with Denis Healey eyebrows that you wished your Leatherman had a handy pair of shears attachment and wore a green checked shirt with a red cravat, a brown check tweed jacket was draped over the back of his chair.

"I hope you're not 'ere to pinch our village sign," said the white haired chap in the crimson shirt who was sat at the same table as Eyebrows, and his grey eyes darted about the bar area to see if we'd actually brought the village sign in with us.

"It won't be the first time," replied Batman...sorry, Hugo.

"We passed it a mile or so back, but I think the bus driver would have something to say if we tried to get on the bus back to Loughborough carrying your village sign," I replied with a grin. With that the villagers continued what they had been doing before we entered.

"I'm just off to the toilet, get the drinks in," I said handing Hugo a twenty pound note.

"Tell me what you want to drink first, Bert?" I followed Hugo to the bar which had a fruit machine in the corner. Above the optics was a sign saying, 'Roger and Manda welcome you to The Gotham Arms'.

"Yes gents," said the man behind the bar who was tall, athletic and looked like a middle-aged tanned surfer dude with longish blonde hair flecked grey at the temples and a toothpaste advert smile and wore a pink polo shirt with the collar up, who was probably Roger. I quickly scanned the variety of beers available: Doom Bar, Pedigree, Timothy Taylor's Landlord, Wainwright and Tiger. "Yeah, I'll try a pint of Landlord, Hugo."

"Two pints of Landlord please landlord," Hugo said to Roger, as I went to find the toilet.

I returned after a few minutes to find Hugo entering what I took to be the lounge which had blue walls with black and white framed photos of what looked like Gotham in the early twentieth-century, either side of which were red plush seats against the walls with alternatively two and four-seater sized wooden tables with dark brown leather high backed chairs which all sat on a dark blue patterned carpet. There was a TV in the far corner, but it wasn't switched on.

Underneath the TV sat an elderly woman with short white hair wearing a grass green roll-necked top, tucking into fish and chips, on spotting Hugo her eyes widened as they telescoped over the top of the tortoise-shell coloured rims of her owlish glasses, and after an economical shake of her head, impaled a ketchup covered chip with her fork and popped it into her mouth.

In the opposite corner was a much younger woman with shoulder length auburn hair dressed in a flamingo pink trouser suit with a lighter pink top and was knitting something from a pink ball of wool, when she wasn't texting on her mobile phone or drinking what looked like orange juice from a tall glass, she looked at Hugo, smiled and then resumed her knitting.

"How come wherever we go, there are always strange people?" Hugo whispered.

"Says the man in the Batman costume," I shot back with a smile. "Denise was like that, wherever we went she was like a magnet for strange people to come over and chat to her when we were trying to eat or have a drink. She used to tell me off when I told them to hop it!"

"They were only being friendly," Hugo replied with a snigger.

"Yeah right, I said as Hugo gave me in slummy what was left of my twenty pound note. "I won't be coming here too often if that's the price of two beers!"

"I've ordered us some food as well, Bert."

"Care to tell me what you've ordered?"

"Grilled smoked cheese and honey glazed ham on ciabatta bread which comes with fries."

"Mmm, sounds very nice," I answered putting away the slummy in my pocket and taking a sip of my pint.

"Well I'm off to the toilets now to change, Bert."

"Jolly dee."

"There's a beer garden out the back, Bert," Hugo said appearing as his normal self in a colourful palm tree decorated blue Hawaiian shirt with khaki coloured cargo pants and his Timberland boots.

"Lead on," I replied grabbing both pints and followed Hugo out into the sunshine. The beer 'garden' had wooden decking and had round wooden picnic tables with blue Pepsi parasols in the centre, and four individual curved bench seats all mounted on a concrete base.

"Two cheese and ham ciabatta with fries," shouted Roger, who we could see was wearing a pair of fawn coloured shorts and brown sandals to accompany his pink top. "Over here," hailed Hugo, raising his right hand. "Enjoy," said Roger as he set down the plates.

We tucked into our delicious lunch and passed away the afternoon basking in the sunshine and drinking Timothy Taylor's Landlord beer.

Chapter Two

Monday morning was bright and warm as I opened the right hand side of my lounge window, I normally liked to open both sides but I had recently lost the key that fitted the lock in the handles and the left one was stuck in the locked position, luckily the right side had been open at the time.

I had a quick shower and coffee, checked I had my wallet and house keys, grabbed my black ex-RAF holdall and walked the ten minute journey to the Beaufort bus station to catch the 74 to St. Margaret's Bus Station in Leicester.

After an uneventful journey into Leicester, I found Hugo in the bus station café, sat at a table with a coffee and reading the *Metro* free newspaper. "Morning Hugo."

"Morning Bert, how are you?"

"What!" I said, 'You'll have to speak up, because I can't hear anything because of that loud shirt!"

"What's wrong with it?"

"When do the circus want it back?" I joked, as it looked like he was wearing a shirt made from a Jackson Pollock painting.

"Har de bloody har, Bert, very droll."

"Yeah, I'm good thanks, Hugo, and you?"

"The sun is shining; the birds are singing, and I'm looking forward to our trip to Wales. I've already ordered the all-day breakfast," replied Hugo sounding quite jolly.

"Have you ever been to Wales before, Hugo?"

"No never, Bert."

"Oh right, how did you get here?"

"Got the 26 to Leicester, then I cut through the Haymarket, walked down Church Gate and turned right into Gravel Street."

"If you'd have got the 74, it would've dropped you off right outside."

"Swings and roundabouts, Bert."

Blodwyn Pugh was a good friend of mine who I had known since the mid-nineties when we had served together in the RAF.

Hugo, Blodwyn and I had finally been able to arrange for four days in September, when we would all be free from all other commitments and Hugo and I could go and visit Blodwyn before she moved from North Cornelly into her new home in Ynysddu, which had been the main reason we hadn't been able to visit sooner, as the move because of one thing and another was taking longer than expected, plus the Doctor Who Experience exhibition in Cardiff, which Hugo had long wished to visit, was closing after its five-year lease expired on the 9th of September and Blodwyn had managed to get tickets for Tuesday 4th of September.

"Think I'll have the all-day breakfast as well," I said, putting my holdall down next to the table and then walked over to the counter.

"Can I help?" Said the woman in the black polo shirt with the cheery face, which was devoid of make-up and had brown hair streaked blonde, tied back in a ponytail. "Can I have the all-day breakfast and a cup of coffee please?"

"Tomatoes or beans?"

"Beans please."

"£6.89 please," the woman said, checking the menu board for the prices. 'Do you take sugar?'

"No thanks." She then put the coffee on the counter and gave me a ticket with the number eight on it. I walked back over to the table, placed my coffee down and took off my zippered, waist length blue jacket and draped it on the back of the chair before sitting down opposite Hugo, facing the back of the café which was trapezoid shaped.

"What's your number Hugo?"

"Five," he said looking up from the newspaper and eyeing his ticket. The rectangular wooden tables had rounded edges and came in different lengths to accommodate either two, four or six of the blue plastic seats. We were sat at a four-seat table.

The left-hand side of the café was glazed and afforded a view of the concourse and the bus bays. On the right was a waist high wall, topped with black wrought iron railings which separated the café from the walkway which led out to Gravel Street. On the wall next to the chiller cabinet which held drinks, fruit and sandwiches was a framed picture of the classic railway poster 'Skegness is SO bracing' with a picture of a jolly fisherman prancing along the beach.

On the table opposite us sat a young Chinese couple, who were sharing a plate of omelette and chips and were taking turns to feed each other.

"Two all-day breakfasts," the woman shouted from the counter. As I was the nearest, I went up to get them, placed them on the table and returned to the counter to pick up the two plates of toast which also had the knives and forks on them. I sat down and then immediately got up again to fetch the salt and brown sauce from the counter.

The all-day breakfast consisted of one egg, one sausage, two rashers of bacon, beans and a slice of toast and fried bread both cut diagonally in half. On the rare occasions that cafes served fried bread, I liked to put my egg on one half and the beans on the other half. Hugo and I ate our enjoyable breakfasts in silence before talking again. "What time is the coach again, Bert?"

"11:15," I replied as Hugo looked at his mobile phone.

"Plenty of time, do you want to have a look at the paper?"

"I had a flick through it on the bus, thanks, d'ya want another coffee?"

"Yes, why not, Bert." I got up from the table and walked over to the counter.

"What can I get you?" asked the same woman.

"Two coffees please."

"£3.80 please." I paid the woman and returned to the table.

"When we get to Cardiff, whatever you do, do *not* call Blodwyn, Blodwyn to her face!"

"Why, what will happen, Bert?"

"She'll only rip your arm off and beat you over the head with the soggy end, and it's no use running away as you'll only die tired!" Hugo looked at me with concern. "Nah, she won't do anything like that, but she doesn't like the name," as I don't like being called Richard, I said laughing.

"What about Blod?"

"No, Hugo, she just likes to be called B!"

"Is that B-e-e or B-e-a?" Hugo said spelling out the names.

"No, just the capital letter B!"

"What about Bertie?"

"Be it on your own head, Hugo, you've been warned!"

"That's funny, Bert."

"Come again?"

"You said, 'B' it on your own head," replied Hugo making the annoying 'rabbit ears' sign with his fingers.

"Hilarious, Hugo."

"What's her partner's name?"

"Bu, or summat like that, I think it's French, but everyone just calls her Bu."

"So, B and Bu, then?"

"Yes, Hugo."

Coffees finished, we visited the toilets and came out onto Gravel Street to await the coach.

Chapter Three

After only a few minutes of sitting on the metal benches, the Service NX 339 coach came into view and went past us and came to a stop at Z Bay 1 at the end of the street. Hugo and I picked up our bags and walked the short distance to the stop, where we joined the other waiting passengers.

Hugo suddenly stopped and exclaimed "Blimey, it's David Soul!" I looked at the driver as he stepped off the coach. He was dressed in a white shirt with a red tie over which was a Hi-Viz yellow vest, and he *did* actually look like David Soul with his silvered hair, sunglasses and a white goatee beard. The driver smiled thinly and rolled his eyes as if to say, 'I've never heard that before'. He bent down and opened up the baggage doors and pulled out the bags and suitcases from the capacious hold for the passengers alighting at Leicester, then began to check the tickets of the passengers getting on and put a chalk mark on their luggage before stowing it in the hold.

The two women in the queue ahead of us I overhead were going to Taunton. I noticed on the side of the coach when we were waiting to board that the coach's final destination was Westward Ho!, which is a seaside village in Devon, and is famous for being the only place name in Britain to have an exclamation mark.

I gave the driver my e-ticket which I had printed off in the library last week when I had made the booking and with a handheld device, he scanned the code on it and took our bags. We then climbed the steps and Hugo found us some seats in the middle of the coach on the right-hand side in front of the toilet. We fastened our seat belts and after a safety brief by the driver, the coach left at exactly 11:15.

"I don't think much of the in-coach entertainment, Hugo," I said pointing to the front of the coach where in the middle sat a TV screen showing the road ahead.

"Nor me, this will get everyone going," Hugo winked as he began to sing 'Silver Lady' by David Soul, which had topped the

UK pop chart in 1977, and he had also sung the song while driving a coach in an advert for National Express.

The passengers in the seats ahead of us, either turned their heads round or turned round fully in their seats to get a better view of who was singing, while others sang along from the front and back. Even the driver was looking at Hugo through the rear-view mirror and singing along.

After Hugo had finished his impromptu performance, the whole coach clapped and cheered his singing. Hugo then stood up and held out his hands. "Thank you, and I mean that most sincerely, folks," said Hugo in the Canadian accent of Hughie Green, and then sat back down.

"Do you want to have a look at the paper, Bert? I see Hamilton won the Italian Grand Prix yesterday."

"No thanks again, I watched it on the TV last night. He started the race seven points behind championship leader Sebastian Vettell, and finished three points ahead, as Vettell came third, and now goes forward in two weeks' time to the Singapore Grand Prix as the championship leader plus he has overtaken Michael Schumacher's record of sixty-eight pole positions. I'm well chuffed Hugo, and with only seven races to go, I think Hamilton has turned a corner and has a good chance at winning the championship this season."

"Ooh, very nice, Bert," said Hugo in his Cissy voice.

The coach wound its way through the city centre and then turned onto the exceedingly long Narborough Road, dodged around the Fosse Shopping Park and then onto the A5460.

"Have you ever heard of quark?"

"Yes, he's the Ferengi owner of the bar in *Star Trek Deep: Space 9*, Bert."

"Yeah, he is, but anyway at the birthday party I told you I went to the other week, there was this woman who was on a diet. There was plenty of buffet food, but she had brought her own which was in a small one-person picnic basket. She had a chicken salad wrap and a small plastic tub of summat, which she told me was chocolate flavoured quark."

"Chocolate flavoured quark, what on earth is that!" Exclaimed Hugo.

"It's some kind of low fat dairy product."

"Sounds lovely," Hugo replied as he struggled to plug in his mobile phone charger in the plug socket at the bottom of the gap between the seats.

"Yeah delicious I'm sure, there was none of this quark, quinoa or couscous when we were young it was either rice or tinned spaghetti!"

"I think the most exotic thing we had to eat when we were kids was a pomegranate or a coconut, Bert."

"Yeah, but the pomegranates were a real pain to eat with having to stick a pin in the individual seeds, it took ages just to eat half a one!"

"Where do they come from, Bert?"

"I honestly have no idea, we can ask Blodwyn to look it up on her phone," I replied looking out of the window as the coach turned onto the M69.

"Has your Shanny stopped smoking yet?" I overheard the brunette woman in the seat ahead of me say to her friend.

"Yes, she has actually," replied her blonde spiky haired friend who was sat by the window.

"Really?"

"Yes, it's been about three months now, but she'll probably restart once the baby's born."

"Oh, I hope she doesn't."

"Me too."

The coach joined the M6 at Junction 2, and we were making good time along the motorway, and on the right we passed in rapid succession The Fort Shopping Park, which was originally constructed during the First World War as the huge and iconic Fort Dunlop building, manufacturing rubber tyres and at one time it was the world's largest factory; and then Villa Park, the stadium of Aston Villa Football Club.

"Did you know there's a simple task that robots, no matter how sophisticated they are, cannot perform, which a typical six-year old can do?"

"What's that then, Bert?' Hugo replied, pondering the question.

"Tie shoelaces!"

"I didn't know robots wore lace-up shoes."

"Hmmm," I muttered, shaking my head.

"Bert has got a pet goat, but it's been unable to perform, so the vet gave him some tablets to arouse the goat's virility. What are they like, Ada? I don't know, but Bert says they taste of peppermint!" Said Hugo, doing another Cissy and Ada sketch and laughing himself silly, which made me laugh even more.

Turning off the motorway, the coach embarked on a slow stop-start journey through Birmingham city centre, along the way passing the ultramodern looking Selfridges department store on the right which contrasted greatly to the Portland stone façade of the turn of the last century, Digbeth Police Station on the left, and then after a few more turns we arrived at Digbeth Coach Station at 12:25, just five minutes late. We filed off the coach with the all the other passengers as the driver was having a rest stop. We picked up our bags off the floor and headed into the station.

Hugo headed to the information desk to ask what bay the Cardiff coach would be leaving from and I headed to the toilet. I had to dig out 30p from my pocket for the privilege, and then job done I walked to the Whistle Stop shop to get the coffees. It was one of those self-service coffee machines. I decided to have a flat white for a change and took a large size cup and placed it in position and pressed my selection. After a minute or two the cup was full, and then I repeated the action for Hugo, but selected a latte. I put a lid on both cups and took them to the till and handed over £5.20.

"The coach leaves from Bay 9/10 at one o'clock, Bert."

"Jolly dee," I replied handing the coffee to Hugo. "I got you a latte."

"Cheers, Bert."

We wandered along the concourse until we found Bay 9/10 and sat down on the metal seats. I looked up at the destination board and read that the 13:00 coach to Swansea called at Newport (S. Wales), Cardiff (Sophia Gardens) which was our stop, and then the coach carried on to Bridgend-Sarn, Port Talbot and Swansea.

Chapter Four

The coach pulled out at 13:06, six minutes behind schedule and the driver gave us the same safety brief as on the previous coach. As we travelled out of the city along Hagley Road which had lots of hotels and B & B's along both sides, one of which my ex-wife Denise and I had spent our wedding night in before travelling to London the next day for our honeymoon.

Further along on the right we passed Lightwoods Park with its restored Grade II listed Bandstand, which was used to host wedding ceremonies, then I noticed there were lots of signboards advertising Cadbury World. "Have you ever been to Cadbury World?"

"No, I haven't, Bert, is it any good?"

"Yeah, if you love chocolate it's brilliant. I took Denise there one year for her birthday. It was a bit of a walk from Bournville train station but we both really enjoyed it. You get lots of chocolate to sample on your way around the site and you could spend a fortune in the shop on chocolate and other merchandise."

"Bloody hell, Bert, someone's dropped an eggy guffer," Hugo whispered, putting his hand up to cover his nose and mouth

"Gawd, that's a global killer! It's not you is it?" I whispered back, pinching my nose with my right thumb and forefinger.

"No, it isn't!" Hugo countered sounding unamused through his half covered face. "I think it might be the woman reading the magazine opposite us." I furtively looked in her direction, but the elderly woman with the short, tightly curled grey hair just sat there nonchalantly with her head down studying her *Puzzler* magazine, looking like butter wouldn't melt in her mouth.

In the seats ahead of the flatulent woman, sat two young Asian girls who were making a meal out of wrapping a large cardboard box in flowery gift-wrap in the confines of their seats. They had brought Sellotape with them but had to use the straight edge of the laminated coach safety guide to cut the paper. The wrapped parcel was then placed in the overhead rack and then another parcel of the same size was brought down to be wrapped in the same way.

The coach travelled along the A456 and joined the M5 at Junction 3. On the left we passed Frankley Services, which I never expected to see again in my life, though it holds very fond memories for me. A RAF buddy of mine who lived in Stafford used to drop me off there every Friday evening after we motored up from Wiltshire and then would pick me back up again on Sunday evening. Denise, who was my fiancé at the time, would then pick me up from the services and take me back to her home in Brierley Hill for the weekend.

"Fancy a Revel?" Hugo asked opening a bag of them.

"Yes please!"

"Hold out your hand." Hugo poured about five or six into my palm and I put them all into my mouth at the same time getting hits of chocolate mixed with coffee, orange and toffee.

"Do you know lovers of Revels are called 'Revellers', Bert?"

"No, but I take it you're a Reveller?"

"Oh yesss," replied Hugo imitating Jacqueline Stewart from the *Benidorm* TV series.

The coach left the M5 at Junction 6 and pulled into the car park of the Sixways Stadium, home to the Worcester Warriors Rugby Football Team. One woman got off and nobody got on and the coach re-joined the M5.

I became engrossed in the conversation between the two men in the seats behind us, who were talking about a former work colleague. "Yeah he used to pinch food out of the fridge," said the man in the aisle seat behind me. "I can believe it, I remember he told me a story once, about how his son had had his bike stolen, and one day as he was walking home from work he saw his son's bike in the front garden of someone that lived in the next street and took it home with him. He told his son he had found his bike, and the son on looking at it, told him it wasn't his bike! Fair play to Clint, he returned the bike back to where he had taken it from, but the man who lived there saw him out of the window and came out and berated him for stealing *his* son's bike. Clint just turned round and said, 'Don't push it pal' and stormed off," the man in the window seat behind Hugo replied.

"That's Clint!" Aisle seat man declared.

Turning onto the M50, we headed towards South Wales and at Ross-on-Wye the coach turned onto the A40 to Monmouth. I looked at the time on my mobile phone, it was 14:42. Blodwyn had asked me to text her when we were an hour away from the coach station in Cardiff, I tapped on the keys that we were due in at 15:35. After a minute my phone 'pinged' to say that Blodwyn was on her way. I acknowledged her text with a 'smiley face' emoticon.

I could feel the coach rapidly slowing. "What's happening?" I said looking up from my mobile phone and looking out of the window.

"We're just approaching a red light, Bert." I looked out the windows, the red brick Monmouth School for Boys was on the right, and a bridge over the Wye River was on the left.

"We'll soon be at Newport, then the next stop is Cardiff."

"Good," replied Hugo rubbing his hands together.

We travelled along the A449 and then the M4 before the run in to the Newport stop which was opposite the Friars Walk Shopping Centre where the coach came to a halt at 15:06. The two Asian girls retrieved their wrapped gifts from the overhead rack and got off at the stop, which looked like a regular bus stop but with a sign saying, 'National Express Coaches Only'. I took the opportunity as the coach was stationary to visit the toilet, as when it was on the move it was very difficult to keep your aim on the target, so to speak. Talk about small, it was like standing in an upright coffin. I'd just returned to my seat as the driver climbed aboard.

The coach re-joined the M4 then travelled along the A48(M) and the A48, then snaked its way around the suburbs of Cardiff before arriving at the open air Sophia Gardens Coach Station bang on time at 15:35. The gardens were a large public park close to the city centre and also home to Glamorgan County Cricket Club.

We queued to get off the coach with quite a few other passengers and by the time we got off the coach our bags had already been off loaded, we picked them up and started to look around for any sign of Blodwyn.

"Watch out for a silver, D reg Opel Manta Berlinetta."

"What the hell does one of them look like, Bert?"

"A Vauxhall Cavalier, oh, and the most noticeable thing about it is, the photon torpedo on the roof."

"Photon torpedo?" Queried Hugo looking puzzled.

"Yeah, one of them streamlined rooftop luggage container thingies."

"Okaaay, Bert," answered Hugo, still none the wiser.

After about five minutes my phone began to ring. "Where are you?" Blodwyn asked.

"We're just by the line of coaches," I replied. The phone line went silent for a few seconds.

"Yes, I can see you now, I'm on the road at the back of the coaches, I'm outside the car waving at you." I scanned the line of cars along the roadway and saw her waving with both hands. Hugo and I made our way to her car where Blodwyn and I hugged each other. "B this is Hugo."

"Pleased to meet you, Hugo," Blodwyn replied, giving him a hug.

"I'm very pleased to meet you B." We put our bags in the back of her car, and on closing the boot I noticed there was a Swansea City Football Club sticker attached on the right side just above the bumper. "Shotgun," I announced just before we got in the car, and Hugo got in the back with me sitting in the passenger seat next to Blodwyn. "What's shotgun?" Blodwyn asked.

"Haven't you seen *The Inbetweeners* TV series?"

"I can't say I have."

"Oh, it's about four school friends, one of whom has a car, and the first one to say 'shotgun' out of the other three gets to sit in the front."

"Sounds very juvenile, Rick."

"It is."

Blodwyn was a vivacious forty-seven-year-old of medium height with short blonde hair. Her face was plain looking with a small nose and mouth that wore the minimum of make-up. But the one thing that made her stand out from the crowd was her eyes. At first you could not quite put your finger on it, was it a trick of the light or contact lenses? No, she actually had different coloured eyes! The left iris was an icy blue, and the right iris was jade green. She wore a black roll-up brimmed hat perched jauntily on the back of her head and a short black leather biker jacket with quilted stitching on the shoulders and upper sleeves with zippered cuffs over a knee length black-and-white horizontally striped dress worn with a pale blue scarf with silver flecks, black opaque tights and classic black court shoes. She looked lean and fit from all the half-marathons and cycle charity events she took part in.

"Where's Bu?" I enquired.

"She's at home, packing her stuff as she's back on shift tomorrow morning for four days."

"That's a shame."

"Yes, it is, but she'll come out with us for a meal out tonight, then travel back after the meal.

"That'll be nice."

"Yes, anyway, how was your journey?" Blodwyn asked as she turned down the volume on the radio that was currently playing Blondie's 'Hangin' on the Telephone'.

"Yeah, it was good thanks apart from a passenger letting one rip, the journey to Birmingham was just over an hour and Hugo was entertaining the passengers with his rendition of 'Silver Lady' which was quite good."

"The David Soul classic?" Blodwyn asked.

"Yeah, that's right, and it also featured in an advert for National Express."

"You must admit though, Bert, the driver did look like David Soul!"

"Yeah, he did actually, I have to say. Then we had a forty-minute wait at Birmingham where we had a coffee, and then it took two and a half hours to get to Cardiff."

"Not too bad a journey then, Rick."

"No, the time passed quite quickly."

"Bert tells me you have been to the Doctor Who Experience a few times, B."

"Yes, over the five years, it's a brilliant exhibition, I shall miss it when it closes for good on Saturday. Are you looking forward to going tomorrow?"

"I sure am, and I think Bert is too."

"Yeah, I am actually." I replied.

"What do you think about the next Doctor Who being a woman, B?" Asked Hugo.

"I'm not sure yet what she will be like, but I am willing to give her a chance, but no one will ever be as good as the Tenth Doctor."

"I take it you liked David Tennant then, B?"

"Oh yes," Blodwyn replied looking at Hugo through the rear view mirror with a twinkle in her eye.

"I grew up with Jon Pertwee and Tom Baker, who I think were the best doctors," I said.

"Yes me too, has your car got a name, B?"

"I'm not going to lie to you, Hugo…no, sorry."

Chapter Five

I must have dozed off in the car, as when I came round we had come to a halt on Blodwyn's gravel driveway. We retrieved our bags from the boot and followed Blodwyn into her house by the side door and walked through the kitchen into the lounge which was warm and spacious with pale blue walls covered in pictures, mostly of treasured former pets and had walnut laminate flooring with a large rectangular rug covered in a square pattern of turquoise, purple, yellow and beige pastel colours. A 50-inch LED TV sat on a black and chrome stand. A coffee coloured 3 x 2 corner sofa with multi-coloured cushions occupied the far corner of the room with a glass topped coffee table with wood surround and ornate wrought iron legs positioned in front of it, in the opposite corner was a wooden DVD and CD storage unit, filled to capacity.

"This is Bu," Blodwyn said as Bu entered the room.

"Give me a *cwtch* then," Bu said.

"What's a *cwtch*? I replied.

"I will show you," she said walking towards me and threw her arms around me and gave me a big hug.

"Is Bu short for anything?" Asked Hugo.

"Bufoy, it's French."

"*Bonsoir, comment allez vous mon chou,*" said Hugo as he hugged Bu, and kissed her on both cheeks.

"The only French thing about me is my name, Hugo."

"He thinks he's Pepe Le Pew," I said laughing.

"I've heard a lot about you, Rick," Bu said with a voice like a purring kitten and a gleam in her eye. Bufoy 'Bu' Churchwell, I would say was around the same age as Blodwyn but taller, strikingly attractive with a touch of the exotic about her, with designer glasses worn over large hazel coloured eyes with sculpted eyebrows, she had cherry coloured lips and long shiny black hair that was parted in the middle, the left side was brushed over the back of her shoulder, while the right side fell over her eye and down the front of her shoulder like a sultry 1940's film star. She wore a tight fitting plain white T-shirt tucked into black leather trousers with a black belt that had a double row of metal studs along its length and a pair of what looked like black leather biker boots. I noticed she had a tattoo on the outside edge of her left hand that said Breathe.

"So, let me get this straight, your name is Blodwyn, but you like to be called B," Hugo said, mouthing the word Blodwyn instead of saying it aloud.

"Yes."

"And your name is Bufoy, but you like to be called Bu."

"That's correct."

"And you're both firefighters."

"Correct," they both said together.

"So, what's the rest of your watch called, Barney McGrew, Cuthbert, Dibble and Grubb?" A ripple of laughter spread between the four of us.

"We don't actually work at the same station," answered Bu still laughing. "I work for Mid and West Wales Fire and Rescue Service in Swansea and B works for South Wales Fire and Rescue Service in Cardiff."

"Would you both like a drink?" Blodwyn interjected.

"Coffee please," I replied.

"Coffee for me too thanks," answered Hugo

"NATO standard?" asked Blodwyn with a smile.

"You're such a cabbage, B, just milk for me thanks and Hugo takes his NATO standard." I called out as she disappeared into the kitchen. A cabbage was a forces term for anybody who used military jargon in normal conversation or did anything remotely military in a non-military situation.

"What's NATO standard, Bert?" Enquired Hugo.

"Tea or coffee, with milk and two sugars."

"Just the way I like it, I'll have to remember NATO standard."

Hugo and I sat down on the sofa and on the coffee table in front of us was a copy of the *Radio Times* which featured Sir Bruce Forsythe on the cover together with a large spiral bound scrapbook with a map design on the cover. A white sticker had been placed centrally on the front, and in black marker pen it read 'The Beast of Black Woods'. Out of curiosity, I put my glasses on and picked it up, and on opening it I found it contained articles that had been mainly cut out of the local newspaper, the *South Wales Star* and gummed down onto the thick paper pages of sightings of what had been dubbed 'The Beast of Black Woods'. I read through a few of the articles and noted with interest the last one was dated only three days ago, with the headline 'Beast Spotted Again'. The article told the experience of former nurse Mrs Ffion Williams, 63, of South Cornelly who had been walking her dog Bonnie, a Yorkshire Terrier along the various trails in the wood when it started to bark and then bare its teeth at something further along the trail and that's when she witnessed a tall, scaly creature on two legs disappear into the trees. I then passed the scrapbook to Hugo to read.

"What's this all about B?" I said indicating the scrapbook.

"I have known about the legend since I was a child, and over the past few years I've just collected together all the articles in the local newspapers about *our* local monster The Beast of Black Woods," Blodwyn replied in a scary voice as she set down the coffees on the table.

"Rather like The Beast of Bodmin," said Hugo.

"Yes, similar. But I don't think the people round here would know the beast if it poked them in the eye!"

"Why is that?" I enquired, taking a cautious sip of my coffee.

"Well, according to the 'eyewitness' reports in the articles you have there, it ranges from four feet to seven feet tall; walks on two, four or six legs; has one or two eyes that are either red, green, yellow or black; is either hairy, furry or has skin like a lizard, has lupine features, has either a tail or no tail, fangs, tusks, horns or huge teeth dripping with blood, and is responsible for attacks on sheep, and some even say it has wings! Some mischief makers have even used large stuffed toys or made painted cardboard cut-outs of lions, tigers and other big cats, and then placed them on top of walls, in fields or left them out in any other open space, so passers-by or helicopter pilots think they are real and contact the police, and have also taken photos of them and then posted them on the internet as real big cats."

"So, I read," I replied. "But it's a well-documented fact that eyewitness reports can be wildly inaccurate or even biased."

"Maybe it's a shape shifter, said Hugo looking up from the scrapbook. "I think I'd like to visit Black Woods, Bert, and see what's happening in there."

"It's only twenty minutes away by car," added Blodwyn.

"Have you ever been to Black Woods, B?"

"Yes, a few times, Rick, but I've never seen anything remotely resembling a beast or anything else, though I have sensed that there *is* something following me, when I have been out jogging."

"Have you been to Black Woods, Bu?"

"No, never, though I have read B's scrapbook, Rick."

"Is Black Woods the proper name for it, or does it have another less sinister name?" Asked Hugo.

"It probably does have a proper name, but everyone since I can remember as a child, just calls it Black Woods."

"We've got to go and have a look for ourselves, Bert. It shouldn't be too hard to spot, all we are looking for is a winged, seven foot, six-legged furry lizard with blood stained tusks!"

"Hmm," I mused.

"If you've finished your drinks, I'll show you to your rooms where you can freshen up before we go out for something to eat, I've booked a table at the local pub for 7pm." We drained our cups, collected our bags and followed Blodwyn up the stairs. "This is the toilet with bath and shower, and I've left some towels on your beds for you to use," Blodwyn said pushing the door open of the room directly in front of us.

"Okay, I said as I looked into the white and spotless room.

"This is your room, Hugo," Blodwyn said opening the door of the next room on the right.

"Thanks, B," Hugo replied, as he vanished inside. Blodwyn and I did an 'about face' and turned right and walked along the landing. "And this is your room, Rick," Blodwyn said opening the door of the next room, "Unless…you'd like to share with Hugo,' Blodwyn added with a mischievous smile.

"No, no, this room is fine, thank you, B."

"The end room is mine and Bu's, I'll see you downstairs, Blodwyn replied, smiling.

The bedroom was bright and airy with magnolia walls, a white ceiling and a wooden floor with a multi coloured rug in front of a wooden framed double bed that had a vertical blue and white striped duvet cover and two plump pillows, the covers of which were in the same pattern. A wooden three-drawer chest of drawers acted as a bedside table while a matching rectangular wooden six-over-two chest of drawers sat along the near wall. A single window occupied the far wall overlooking the driveway, with the other three walls decorated with pictures of dogs.

I unzipped my holdall and took out the contents and laid them out on the bed; shirts, trousers, socks, underwear, soap bag etc., and a bag of James Patterson books I had read. Blodwyn and I regularly sent each other books in the post we had read, but as I knew I would be coming to visit her shortly I had saved the last batch to bring with me.

I stripped to the waist and took my washbag and the towel Blodwyn had provided to the bathroom opposite and brushed my teeth and hair and sprayed on some antiperspirant before returning to the bedroom to put on a fresh shirt in a vibrant blue colour and after putting my clothing away in the chest of drawers I was good to go. I grabbed the bag of books and joined Blodwyn and Bu in the living room.

"Here's some James Patterson books that I have read," I said, handing over the plastic bag to Blodwyn.

"Thanks, Rick. Did you read those Tess Gerritsen books I sent you?"

"I've read the first two, *The Surgeon* and *The Apprentice*. They're a lot darker than the *Rizzoli and Isles* TV series aren't they?"

"Yes, the series is a lot lighter and has more humour."

"How did you two meet?" asked Hugo, on joining us back in the living room having also freshened up and changed his shirt for a red Hawaiian design one.

"We met at a Texas concert in Cardiff, ooh, must have been two years ago," replied Blodwyn. "Yes, it was in 2015... in the May," added Bu. Both women looked at each other and smiled.

"Is that place that ends in *gogogoch*, anywhere near here B?" Hugo asked.

"*Llanfairpwllgwyngyllgogerychwyrndrobwllllantysiliogogogoch?*"Blodwyn rattled off.

"That's easy for you to say," Hugo said with a laugh.

"No, it's in Anglesey, North Wales," Blodwyn said laughing, "But most people shorten it to *Llanfair PG*".

"Oh, what does it mean in English?" I asked.

"St Mary's church in the hollow of the white hazel near to the fierce whirlpool of St Tysilio of the red cave, or something like that."

"Wow, that's a pretty good description of its whereabouts."

"Yes, and this is the garden," Blodwyn said as she stepped outside the patio doors. I stepped outside to join her and to the right on a paved section stood a Suzuki Marauder GZ125 motorbike.

"Bu's?" I enquired.

"Yes it is, she uses it to commute to and from work."

Calling it a garden, was a bit of an understatement, it was more like a football field, it was huge with four sheds at the far end. "What's in the sheds, B?"

"In shed one," B said, pointing to the one on the extreme left. "There is power tools, fishing stuff, oils and fluids for my car plus nails, screws, etc., shed two, contains all my gardening tools, shed three, has two bicycles in there and shed four, has a 'ride on' petrol mower and is also where I keep my hot tub in the winter."

"Is it a hot tub time machine?"

"Yes, it can be, Hugo."

"Cool, how many can it fit?"

"Bu and I can fit into it quite comfortably, but I suppose four at a push."

"Cosy," replied Hugo, cocking an eyebrow.

Chapter Six

Blodwyn pulled the Opel into the car park of the Prince of Wales bar and restaurant. Bu was already there, standing beside her motorbike and wore an identical leather jacket to Blodwyn's underneath a yellow Hi-Viz vest, plus a black and white scarf, with her white full-face helmet resting on the seat. Taking off her vest, scarf and jacket and grabbing her helmet, Bu placed them in the boot of the Opel, and we all walked through the door of the pub and came into the empty bar room which had a pool table, dartboard and a wall mounted TV showing a football match. "What do you all want to drink?" Hugo asked.

"I'll have a half pint of Caffrey's please, Hugo," said Blodwyn.

"Bu?"

"Can I have a coke please, Hugo."

"Bert?"

"What other bitters have they got?" I replied.

"We've got Doom Bar," said the waitress, who had long black hair tied in a ponytail and wore a plain black T-shirt and black jeans.

"Yes, I'll have a pint of that thanks, Hugo."

"Okay, that's two pints of Doom Bar, a half pint of Caffrey's and a coke please. Does anybody want any crisps?"

"I'll have a bag of cheese and onion," I replied, while Blodwyn and Bu shook their heads.

"And a bag of cheese and onion crisps please."

Drinks poured, I picked up the two pints while Hugo carried the other two drinks and the crisps over to one of the circular wooden tables and we all sat down. I opened the bag of crisps and proffered them to everyone, but they all politely declined.

"A man walks into a bar and asks for a packet of helicopter flavoured crisps, and the barman replies I'm sorry sir, I've only got plain!"

"Have you been saving that one for just this occasion, Rick?" Blodwyn said after a slow flash of smiles from everyone. "It's my standard joke when I'm eating crisps," I replied.

"Fancy a quick game of pool, anybody?" Asked Bu.

"Yeah, we can all have a game, Hugo and I against the firefighters," I replied.

"You're on, rack em up," said Blodwyn.

Hugo put a £1 coin in the slot, collected the one black, seven red and seven yellow balls and arranged them in the prescribed order in the wooden triangular rack, and then took out the black ball from the centre and manoeuvred the rack into position, replaced the black ball, removed the rack carefully and placed the white ball in position and we were ready to play. Hugo took out a coin from his pocket. "Call," Hugo said as he flipped the coin.

"Heads," said Bu, as Hugo caught the tumbling coin in his right hand and flipped it over onto the back of his left hand. "Heads it is," Hugo cried as he took away his right hand, showing us all the 'heads up' coin.

We all took a cue from the rack in the corner and took turns to apply chalk to the tip from the one chalk cube.

Bu bent down and lined up the shot and struck the white ball which rocketed into the red ball at the apex of the triangle, scattering the fifteen balls in all directions and potting both a yellow and a red ball.

"Yellow," declared Bu, electing the colour they were going to play as she stalked around the table like a lion eyeing up a vulnerable wildebeest, looking for the best shot while chalking her cue again. Bu leaned over the table and sliced a yellow into the bottom left hand pocket.

"I think you two have played this game before," I said to the two women.

"Once or twice," replied Bu, with a wink as she stalked around the table again. Squatting down, Bu viewed the balls from table-top height, then stood up, chalked her cue and struck the white ball that hit a yellow ball into a red ball that hit another yellow ball that dropped in the centre left pocket.

"I have a sneaky feeling, Bert that they've got a pool table at their respective fire stations."

"And table football," added Blodwyn.

"We've got a pair of hustlers, Hugo" I added laughing.

Bu laughed as she lined up her next shot, and struck the white ball which struck a yellow ball and looked as if it was going to drop into the bottom right hand pocket, but the ball danced around the pocket but failed to drop in.

I took a mouthful of beer and then walked around the table looking for an easy shot; there was a red over the central left pocket that just needed a nudge to drop in. I lined up the shot and tapped the white ball which slowly rolled into the red and it fell into the pocket more by luck than design. I chalked the cue and wandered round the table for another easy shot. I tried for the red by the top right-hand pocket, but I hit the white ball a bit too hard and it crashed into the red ball causing it to ricochet around the table and come to rest almost touching the black ball.

Blodwyn took a sip of her drink then got up out of her chair and walked around the table, and spying a shot, had to lean right over the table to take it, the white ball had to squeeze past three reds in line astern to strike the yellow which fell into the bottom left pocket. Calculating the next shot, Blodwyn looked down the cue and struck the white ball which rocketed into a yellow but then caught the edge of a red ball and sent it flying into the top right pocket.

Taking a swig of his pint, Hugo got up and walked slowly around the table, "I shall be using the Evelyn Tremble method," said Hugo with a laugh.

"Isn't that for Baccarat?"

"You know your Bond quotes, Bert," Hugo replied with a smile as he moved the chalk out of his way, then bent over and struck the centre red ball from the line of three and potted it into the left centre pocket and then Hugo and I watched in horror as the white ball rebounded off the cushion and struck the black ball and sent it rolling into the opposite pocket. "Are you sure this table *is* level?" Asked Hugo in jest, to which we all laughed.

At that timely point the waitress appeared, to say our table was now ready and we all filed through into the restaurant, which had white walls with wooden beams across the ceiling and subdued lighting. Hugo and I sat side-by-side and Blodwyn and Bu sat opposite at the black rectangular table with black, tall-backed seats.

The waitress appeared again with the menus and gave us one each and then left. "Does anyone fancy a starter? Blodwyn asked, looking around the table.

"I'd rather have a dessert," I answered.

"Me too," added Hugo.

"And me," said Bu.

"Dessert it is then," confirmed Blodwyn.

I looked at the menu and immediately fancied the three-egg omelette with three fillings, which came with home-made chips, peas, salady stuff and a pot of mayo.

"I'm torn between the scampi and the Glamorgan burger," said Blodwyn. I looked at the menu to see what that was, and it was a burger made from leeks, cheese and breadcrumbs served with chips, peas and salady stuff with tartare sauce, *not my idea of a burger* I thought.

"I think I'll have the pie," Hugo said after much deliberation.

"Hmm, yes, Hunter's Chicken for me," said Bu, eventually.

"Are you ready to order?" The waitress asked, returning to our table.

"I'll have the Glamorgan burger please," said Blodwyn.

"Can I have the Hunters Chicken please," answered Bu.

"The omelette, chips and peas please."

"What fillings do you want?" The waitress asked.

"Oh…err…" I picked up the menu and looked at the list of fillings. "Cheese, ham and onion please," I replied. The waitress wrote it down on a note pad and then turned to Hugo.

"What kind of pie is the Chef Pie of the Week?"

"Steak and ale," the waitress replied.

"Nice, can I have it with chips please?" replied Hugo

"Oh, and can we have some garlic bread please," Blodwyn added. The waitress noted it all down on her notepad and then took the menus from each of us and disappeared through the door to the kitchen.

"What's hunters chicken?" Hugo asked Bu.

"It's chicken breast, topped with bacon, cheese and BBQ sauce and comes with chips and peas."

"Very nice," replied Hugo in his Cissy voice.

The waitress returned after a few minutes, "I'm sorry," she said apologetically, looking at Blodwyn, "We've run out of the Glamorgan burgers."

"Oh, okay, I'll have the scampi then," replied Blodwyn. The waitress smiled and returned back through the door. "The scampi was my first choice, but I changed my mind and went for the Glamorgan burger."

After a while the waitress appeared with two plates of food and the garlic bread and set them down in front of the two women and then disappeared through the door and then reappeared with two more plates and set them down in front of Hugo and I. Blodwyn surveyed her plate of scampi, which was accompanied with chips, peas, salady stuff and a slice of lemon.

We all tucked into our meals. "Ooh, that's a bit of alright," said Hugo breaking the silence while imitating Mary Berry and eating another forkful of pie. "I went to a restaurant with seven of my friends and for a laugh we ordered the pan fried octopus."

"What was it like, Hugo?" Bu had to ask; I had heard it many times before.

"It tasted like chicken and everyone got a leg!" Blodwyn and Bu didn't know whether to laugh or cry and sat there looking at Hugo open mouthed. "It's one of Hugo's jokes," I interjected. "Eight people, eight legs."

"Oh, now I get it said Bu," raising a smile while Blodwyn was smiling on the inside, I presumed.

"Is everything okay?" the waitress enquired appearing out of nowhere like the shopkeeper from the *Mr Benn* TV series.

"Yes thank you, can I have another round of drinks as before please," said Blodwyn, the rest of us just nodded our heads in satisfaction.

"Certainly," the waitress replied and walked back through the kitchen door.

"I've just noticed your finger Bu, what happened?" I asked. Bu looked down at the long, slender index finger of her right hand, which was missing the tip. "That was an education, I can tell you, Rick."

"How, so?"

"I learnt my lesson never to stick my finger inside a rabbit cage ever again!" Bu replied with a laugh.

"Ouch!" I replied.

"Must have thought it was a carrot," Hugo added.

"I keep telling her, she should ask for ten percent off when she has her nails done, as she has only nine digits," Blodwyn added. Hugo sniggered like Muttley.

"Did you enjoy that, B?" Asked Hugo, looking at Blodwyn's empty plate.

"I did thank you, Hugo, I'm as full as an egg."

"I don't think I've heard that expression before," I said laughing.

"I borrowed it from a friend," Blodwyn replied with a smile.

"I'd rate mine as a 'Ten from Len'," I said rubbing my stomach. "I've still got room for dessert though."

As if she had heard me, the waitress reappeared with a trayful of drinks and dessert menus and handed them out. I quickly scanned down the list of tasty puds and there it was, my favourite…New York cheesecake!

"I'll have the New York cheesecake please," I said.

"Would you like cream, custard or vanilla ice cream?" The waitress asked.

"Ooh… cream please."

"I'll have the same please," said Bu.

"Hmm…the sticky toffee pudding with ice cream please," Hugo said looking up from the menu.

"Apple pie with ice cream, thank you," Blodwyn answered. Orders taken, the waitress collected the empty plates and menus and disappeared again into the kitchen.

After a few minutes, the waitress returned with the desserts and we all tucked into them.

"I'm going to have to go now, sorry," said Bu reluctantly, after we had all polished off our desserts and got up from her chair. "I've got a bit of a ride to get home for work in the morning; it was very nice meeting you both and I shall look forward to seeing you again, soon."

"It was very nice to meet you too Bu, have a safe journey home," Hugo and I both said.

"Thank you," Bu replied as she came towards us and gave Hugo and I a *cwtch* and a kiss on the cheek and waved as she made for the door. "I'll be back in a minute," said Blodwyn as she accompanied Bu.

Chapter Seven

"Morning Bert," said Hugo, who was sat down on one of the six, slatted-back chairs around the rectangular dark brown, lacquered finish dining table, drinking a cup of coffee, dressed in a mid-blue T-shirt with 'Trust me I'm the Doctor' in five lines underneath an illustration of a TARDIS, a sand coloured pair of cargo pants and his Timberland boots. "Morning Hugo," I replied with a stretch.

"Morning Rick," said Blodwyn sounding chipper, and was also wearing *Doctor Who* apparel in the form of a navy blue cap with 'Keep calm and call The Doctor' in white below a picture of the TARDIS worn with a pure white with black trim Swansea City football shirt, black jeans and trainers.

"Morning, B."

"How did you sleep?"

"Very well, thank you."

The kitchen/dining room had lemon yellow walls with mottled white square floor tiles, under the single window sat a Belfast sink. I hadn't noticed yesterday when we arrived but by the side door was a wooden three-tiered rack that held twelve plus pairs of brightly coloured trainers above which was a row of running medals suspended from their coloured ribbons.

"Coffee?"

"Oh, yes please, B," I replied stifling a yawn, and joined Hugo at the table. "I can see I'm in the company of some hard-core fans," I added.

"Whovians," Hugo responded.

"Is that a bit like 'Trekkies' but for Doctor Who fans?" I teased.

"You know they're called 'Trekkers', Bert."

"I mustn't have got the memo about wearing *Doctor Who* gear today."

"Well we *are* going to the Doctor Who Experience," replied Hugo, putting on his *Doctor Who* raspberry coloured UNIT beret, which made him look a bit effeminate.

"What's the exhibition like, B," I asked.

"It's brilliant, there's a twenty minute walk-through interactive adventure with the Twelfth Doctor which is mainly for children who sometimes get a bit scared, and then you are free to roam the two floors of exhibits which are an absolute treasure trove of sets, costumes, props and other memorabilia which is the largest collection in the world, plus there's a café and a shop. You cannot take photos in the interactive part, but you can everywhere else."

"Brilliant," Hugo answered.

"You do like *Doctor Who*, don't you, Rick?"

"Yeah I do, as I said, I liked the Third and Fourth Doctors the best and of the later classic Doctors adventures, I can only remember one that had Ken Dodd in it and one that had some monster or other that looked like Bertie Basset!"

"Every time I ate liquorice before I went to bed, I always had these really weird dreams," said Hugo.

"What were they about?" Blodwyn replied with a hint of concern in her voice.

"All Sorts!" Hugo exclaimed laughing.

"I thought you were being serious then," Blodwyn said with a smile.

"You'll soon get to know when Hugo's being serious or not, B. Anyway, I much prefer *Red Dwarf*. During the nineties and right up to 2003, my brother Rod and I used to go each year to the *Red Dwarf* 'Dimension Jump' conventions. They were totally mental but great fun with lots of great characters attending who were totally into it *way* too much. All the main cast members would attend together with the writers and special effects guys, it was just a totally great weekend of fun and drinking. I still have a signed print by the artist Colin Howard inscribed 'Keep on smeggin!' and dated 1994. He also did the cover artwork for the BBC *Doctor Who* VHS video tapes."

"I still have a few of them, I only kept them when I bought them again on DVD because of the brilliant cover artwork," said Hugo.

"I remember watching an episode of *Red Dwarf* when the four of them visited *Coronation Street*," said Blodwyn, eating a banana.

"Yeah, 'Back to Earth' it was a three part mini-series and involved a portal which returned the crew back to Earth in 2009, where they discover their adventures are shown as fiction on the popular *Red Dwarf* TV show, but when they find out they're all going to killed off in the final episode, the foursome decide to track down the creator and beg him to change his mind. They travel to the *Coronation Street* set and find Craig Charles in the Rovers Return learning his lines for his taxi driver character, Lloyd Mullaney who tells them where to find the creator. Arriving at the creator's house he tells the crew he has grown tired of them and is then accidently killed by Lister."

"Don't leave B and I in suspenders, Bert, then what happens?"

"Turns out it was all a shared hallucination brought on by a female relative of the Despair Squid from Series V but used joy to stop the crew from fighting it off."

"Oh right," replied Hugo looking none the wiser.

"After the Doctor Who Experience, we can pop across to Cardiff city centre if you like?"

"Have they got a Pandora shop in Cardiff, B?" Hugo asked.

"Yes, in the shopping centre."

"Oh good, I'd like to get Ruth a little something from there."

"I'll show you where it is," replied Blodwyn.

"Did Bu get back alright last night?" I asked, shaking my head as I watched Hugo adjusting the shapeless beret on his head, *Muppet* I thought smiling to myself.

"Yes, she phoned me to say she had, and that she enjoyed the evening and meeting you both," replied Blodwyn.

"That's good, does your phone have a *Doctor Who* ringtone?"

"Yes, it does," Blodwyn replied with a smile.

"Yeah, I thought I heard it ring last night."

"Do you want to have breakfast here or do you want to get something out?" Asked Blodwyn to us both.

"What have you got?" I enquired.

"There's Weetabix Banana, Weetabix Golden Syrup or porridge?" Blodwyn replied.

"We'll get something out," Hugo intervened. I nodded in agreement.

"That's fine by me," said Blodwyn.

We made sure we had everything for the day ahead, left the house and got in the car. Blodwyn reversed the Opel out of the driveway onto the road and we headed for Cardiff.

"I just saw a sign back there for a place called Splott!" Said Hugo

"Yes, it's been featured in an episode of *Torchwood*." Replied Blodwyn.

After about half an hour of driving we reached Cardiff, where there were lots of brown coloured tourist road signs showing white pictograms of a Dalek and an anchor. Blodwyn parked the car in the Mermaid Quay Car Park and before Hugo and I got out we unloaded all our slummy into the circular well next to the gearstick. After Blodwyn paid the fee we walked the short distance to the Cardiff Bay area.

The day was really bright and sunny, with not a cloud in the baby blue sky as we came to on the left, the striking Wales Millennium Centre, which is a performing arts venue, the exterior was a mixture of glass, copper and recycled Welsh slate with giant phrases on the front in Welsh and English.

"The secret entrance to the Torchwood Three Headquarters which was the Cardiff Branch of the Torchwood Institute was located beneath the Water Tower," said Blodwyn pointing to the very tall shimmering silver tower on the right with an irregular stream of water running down its length. "In fact this whole area has regularly been featured in episodes of *Doctor Who* and *Torchwood*."

"Yes, I recognise them," replied Hugo as we walked on past the bronze statue of Cardiff born song writing legend, Ivor Novello. Blodwyn explained we were in Roald Dahl plass, which was a public space used for festivals and other events and was named after Cardiff born author Roald Dahl, who was probably more famous for his popular children's books, but to me, I remembered him for being an RAF fighter pilot during the war who qualified as being an 'ace' for shooting down five enemy aircraft in aerial combat; writing the screenplay for the 1967 James Bond film *You Only Live Twice* and for penning the TV series *Tales of the Unexpected*.

We carried on and came to the black metal railings overlooking Cardiff Bay. "And down there is Ianto's Shrine." We looked down onto the boardwalk to where Blodwyn was pointing to. Ianto Jones was a character in the *Doctor Who* spin-off *Torchwood* series, which was an anagram of *Doctor Who*. I had watched a few episodes here and there, but I wasn't a fan of the show. "He was killed off in the third series, hence the shrine at what was the public entrance to Torchwood Three," added Blodwyn. "Do you want to go down and have a look?"

"It would be rude not to, B," replied Hugo, taking out his mobile phone to take some photos.

We walked down the steps and along the boardwalk up to the wood panelled wall of the impromptu shrine which had sprang up shortly after the death of Ianto and was plastered with flowers, personal notes, photos, poems etc., from people all around the world in tribute to a much loved but fictional character.

"Can you see that blue and grey futuristic looking building over there?" Blodwyn asked, pointing across the bay. Hugo and I looked across with Hugo curling the fingers of both his hands and raised them to his eyes as if he had a pair of binoculars and spied the building Blodwyn was indicating. It was constructed like a large tent with a cover that was stretched over the curved steel beams.

"That's the Doctor Who Experience."

"It looks huge," I replied, looking across the bay.

We climbed back up the steps and came across a very colourful carousel, as it spun around I was able to read the words 'Norman Sayers and Son Presents Popular Welsh Galloping Horses.' "It is said to be the only Welsh themed carousel in the world," Blodwyn explained.

"Very nice, B," I said as we strolled on past the French Gothic Renaissance styled, terracotta stoned Pierhead Building with its ornamental clock tower, which was originally built as the headquarters of the Bute Dock Company and was now an exhibition and historical museum for the glass fronted National Assembly for Wales building which was next door.

Further along Hugo and I were immediately drawn to what looked like the bows of a ship. As we got nearer we could see it was a grey painted steel sculpture of a ship with a human face incorporated into the hull that sat inside a circular mosaic which read around the circumference 'In Memory of the Merchant Seafarers from the ports of Barry, Penarth, Cardiff Who Died in times of War'. On the memorial plaque we read it was the *Merchant Seafarers War Memorial*.

As we carried on walking towards the exhibition along Harbour Drive, I must have strayed too far into the road as I heard a short, sharp toot of a horn. With a start, I immediately moved to the left as 'Sherrie's Whippy' ice cream van passed me with a smiling, attractive blonde at the wheel.

"You've just met Sherrie," Blodwyn said laughing.

"I'd have died happy as I actually like an ice cream, with raspberry sauce and a flake," I replied with a laugh.

Walking on we came across the *Antarctic 100 Memorial* to commemorate the 100th Anniversary of the Age of Antarctic Discovery. The memorial was a sculpture made up of a mosaic of white irregular tiles standing on a compass rose and depicts Captain Robert Falcon Scott and the faces of the rest of his team, man-hauling on their journey towards the South Pole. Scott's ship, the *Terra Nova* left this very spot for his ill-fated second Antarctic Expedition in June 1910.

"And over there is where Roald Dahl was christened and he was named after Captain Scott's great rival in the race to the South Pole, the Norwegian Roald Amundsen." said Blodwyn pointing to the white clapboard with black roof and spire of the Norwegian Church Arts Centre and Norsk Coffee Shop across the way.

"No wonder he's facing away from it and the Norwegian flag!" I remarked.

"Oh yes," exclaimed Hugo."

"It was formerly a church for visiting Norwegian seamen to the port," added Blodwyn. We passed the arts centre and crossed over the bridge which separated the Roath Basin from the Inner Harbour of Cardiff Bay and walked past the stone

Lock Keeper's Cottage with its bright red doors and window frames, after which was a Coffi Co shop, which was a new one on me. It was built from two recycled and converted crimson coloured ISO shipping containers with glazed fronts and an entrance linking the two. "Do you fancy a coffee, as we're a bit early for our time slot?" Blodwyn asked looking at her watch.

"Yeah, Hugo and I are always up for a coffee."

Blodwyn and Hugo went inside to buy the drinks as I desperately needed to use the toilet which was called 'The Throne'. After I had finished I found them sitting outside of the left-hand container which had a gravel base and wooden seats tables that looked as if they had been made from old railway sleepers Outside of the right-hand container was what looked like artificial turf on which were deck chairs. "What's that you've got there B?" I asked.

"It's one of their signature drinks, it's called a Curly Wurly Latte. It's a normal latte with cream, caramel sauce and a piece of Curly Wurly on the top. I've had one before and they are lush."

"Sounds very nice, B."

"I got you a normal latte, Bert, as I know you don't like all the additions."

"Cheers, Hugo, that's great, I replied. I didn't go in for the flavoured syrups, squirty cream and mini marshmallows that the staff try to tempt you with. "What's that you're drinking?"

"It's a Chocolate Orange hot chocolate, have a taste," Hugo replied taking a bite out of a toasted panini.

"Very nice," I said taking a small sip and passing it back quickly.

"I also got you a grilled chicken toasted panini for breakfast, Rick."

"Thank you, what's on yours, B?"

"Tuna and cheese."

"Mmm, tuna and cheese," I replied pulling a face.

After we had finished our drinks and paninis we binned the cups and wrappers and made our way the short distance to the Doctor Who Experience.

"Hello Geoff!" Exclaimed the woman, standing in front of me with her arms wide open. She sounded as though she knew me but hadn't seen me in a while. I stood there looking at her but had never seen this woman before in my life! She had a pale, severe looking face with thin lips and no make-up and her black hair was scraped back into a ponytail. Below her right ear were three crudely tattooed hollow stars. She wore a teal coloured, knee length duffle coat with a black flap-over faux leather handbag that hung heavily on her left hip with the long strap looped around her right shoulder. I think she must have read my thoughts as she slowly lowered her arms.

"Your name's not Geoff is it?"

"No, sorry," I replied slowly shaking my head as her face began to redden and she hurried away. I glanced back at her as she quickly disappeared out of sight and I shook my head again.

Chapter Eight

Walking towards the glass fronted Doctor Who Exhibition, there was a lone silver/blue Dalek patrolling around the front entrance. We waited until it chased after some young lads then quickly nipped in through the doors, put our tickets in the machine and entered the spacious foyer.

Costumes of the Twelfth Doctor, Clara Oswald and a Gallifreyan soldier plus lots of props and a full size red/black Dalek made entirely of Lego were on display, together with signed and dated handprints of the writers, doctors and companions of the show, rather like the forecourt of Grauman's Chinese Theatre in Hollywood. Hugo just couldn't resist laying his hands over those of Tom Baker, the Fourth Doctor, while Blodwyn slipped her petite hands into the handprints done by David Tennant, the Tenth Doctor.

"The monster zone is on the top floor, Hugo announced excitedly as he perused the floor plan of the exhibition.

"You'll enjoy that," said Blodwyn as excited as Hugo.

Our tickets allowed us entry into the Interactive Adventure and we waited in line with about thirty other people in our time slot, which were mostly children with quite a few wearing home-made *Doctor Who* costumes, before being welcomed into the Gallifrey Museum by the female curator, where we are shown the various exhibits, which were in the main from the Doctors past plus costumes of various Time Lords.

While trying to make a connection with the Twelfth Doctor's TARDIS, it's suddenly attacked by the Krynus; a type of Time Squid, and through distortions in time, the museum and the TARDIS become physically linked.

We are then led through a portal in the museum wall into what appears to be the TARDIS Arch-Recon Room and then on into the Console Room where the Doctor invites us all in and we gather around the control console, and through his guidance some of the children in the group got to pilot and land the TARDIS on a strange looking planet.

On leaving the TARDIS we realise to our horror; it has landed on the Dalek home world of Skaro. As we navigate ourselves through a Dalek infested corridor, and then on into a forest of Weeping Angels, members of the group collect two time crystals along the way. A third time crystal is found in the scrapyard of I. M. Foreman, Scrap Merchant.

We all put on 3D glasses, just in time to witness that when the three time crystals are united it causes the Krynus, Daleks and Weeping Angels to be sucked into a swirling vortex and then disappear into outer space.

After the Doctor and the museum curator thank us all for our help in defeating the trio of enemies, we all leave through the scrapyard gate and come out at 76 Totter's Lane, Shoreditch in the East End of London on Saturday 23 November 1963.

"We've only helped the Twelfth Doctor save the universe, Bert!"

"Yeah, we did along with thirty odd others," I replied with a smile.

"It makes a huge difference if you get an enthusiastic curator like that one, but on some of my visits the curators have acted quite bored with it all."

"I would've loved a job like that, B" replied Hugo.

The first exhibit we came across in the huge hall was the First Doctor's Console Room with its hexagonal control console which was seen in the very first episode 'An Unearthly Child', which was broadcast a little later than billed due to news coverage of the assassination of US President John F. Kennedy which had happened the previous day.

Each of its six panels had a particular function and were festooned with 1960's vintage; buttons, knobs, winking lights, switches, levers, dials and gauges with a transparent cylindrical column in the centre which housed the Time Rotor which went up and down like a piston when the TARDIS was in flight.

Nearby a Dalek loitered menacingly in a Skaro shaped doorway, while small groups of Daleks where everywhere together with props housed in transparent cases.

In the corner was a replica of a 1960's TV production set with a winged, man-sized black and white striped butterfly like Menoptra creature, plus newspapers, photos, props, models, blueprints and other ephemera of the First Doctor's era together with a copy of the very first Doctor Who Annual from 1966 which cost 9s 6d.

To the right, the First Doctor's replica TARDIS sat next to a sign which read 'It is forbidden to dump bodies into the river' set against a brick wall.

The TARDIS had been originally designed with a chameleon circuit which enabled it to blend in with its surroundings wherever it landed, but it had become permanently jammed in the guise of a 1950's blue Metropolitan Police public call box.

Nearby was the Fifth Doctor's control console, which retained the same basic shape as the First Doctor's, but all the controls had been upgraded to 1980's cutting edge technology and it now looked very hi-tech.

Next in line was the Fourth Doctor's TARDIS together with the ever popular K-9 intelligent robotic dog, which had a laser blasting nose, and a deck chair resting on a bed of gravel.

"What's with the deck chair," I asked.

"It's probably one of the ones that the Fourth Doctor and Romana II used on Brighton beach accompanied by K-9, in 'The Leisure Hive' story," replied Hugo.

"Oh right, I think Hugo knows more about the classic series while you, B, concentrate on the modern series."

"So between us we have all the answers," laughed Blodwyn.

"Yes, it seems that way. Does Bu like *Doctor Who*?"

"Not really, Rick, she's more into her crime dramas like *Vera*, *Shetland*, *Midsomer Murders* and *Taggart*."

"I absolutely love *Taggart*; I've got all the DVD's and books and would love to go to Glasgow and visit the locations."

"There's been a murda! Is it serious? Well, if you call murda serious…," quipped Hugo laughing, together with Blodwyn and I, as we walked past a Melkur; a calcified living statue with laser beam firing eyes, on our way to the Ninth and Tenth Doctors control console which was radically different from all the previous Doctors consoles. The multi-tier design had wire mesh flooring and was mounted on a raised circular platform.

The whole console had the feeling of being organic and alive, and was grown from coral rather than being constructed and was roughly circular and retained the six panels of controls and glowed a bluey-green colour with coral columns for structural support, while the wiring and cabling looked like it had been installed by a blind man and resembled 'Spaghetti Junction!'

Next on our route sat the Ninth and Tenth Doctors TARDIS, which then led on to a green screen photo booth for visitors to have their photograph taken against a variety of different backgrounds, together with props and clothing you could use. "We've got to have our picture taken!" Hugo exclaimed.

"Why not," I replied.

"It'll be a good souvenir of our day," Blodwyn added.

Hugo chose the Totter's Lane background for our photo and from the props table, picked up a replica Eleventh Doctor's fez, to replace his beret and the Fourth Doctor's long scarf, while Blodwyn and I picked up a sonic screwdriver each.

Hugo draped the scarf over the three of us and stood in the middle with his right hand 'pinkie' in his mouth in imitation of Doctor Evil from the film *Austin Powers; International Man of Mystery*, and Blodwyn and I stood on either side of him and adopted James Bond poses and wielded our sonic screwdrivers like Walther PPK's. Picture taken, Hugo paid the blonde haired woman with the twin plaited ponytails, who printed off three high-resolution copies of our photo there and then, and we walked on to the next exhibit laughing at them.

Hugo took some photos of the Third Doctor's bright yellow, vintage looking roadster called *Bessie,* which he used to gad about in on his earthbound adventures, which was parked up on a stretch of gravel by the stairs which led up to the next floor.

Chapter Nine

We climbed up the stairs and came face-to face with the Face of Boe as we entered the upper hall. Housed in a powered transportable glass fronted life support tank, the Face of Boe was a huge, weathered human like head who communicated by telepathy, and was said to be billions of years old, and who is also reputed to be Captain Jack Harkness. "You could be looking into a mirror, Hugo, what d'ya say B?"

"Woah, don't get me involved," Blodwyn replied holding up her hands, but the flicker of a smile danced in the corners of her mouth. "Cheers, Bert," replied Hugo looking intently at the Face of Boe.

"Anytime," I said, slapping him on the back.

"His eyes look really sad," commented Hugo.

"So would yours be, if you'd seen what the Face of Boe has witnessed over billions of years," replied Blodwyn, placing her outstretched palm on the glass as if telepathically communicating with the Boekind.

To the right was a line-up of modern monsters and aliens.

"This is what I've been looking forward to!" Hugo cried, taking photos of anything and everything monster related on his mobile phone. As we walked along the row we encountered a Clockwork ship repair droid, flamboyantly dressed in French eighteenth-century clothing complete with what looked like a colourful full face Venetian mask and a wig; a Scarecrow, one of a horde of scary looking animated henchman made of sacking and straw to do the bidding of the alien Family of Blood; an amphibious Hath, which had a human looking body and a fish-like head with what looked like a vial of green liquid in its mouth to breathe through, dressed in military fatigues and a tactical vest; a Sycorax, a spacefaring ancient warrior tribe that wore a bone like mask to hide their gruesome faces; a Silent of The Silence, a sinister religious order of black suited, tall and spindly humanoids with bulbous bony heads, deep set eyes with a screaming expression in place of a mouth, which were based on the famous Edvard Munch painting *The Scream*. If you saw a Silent you would remember all previous sightings of them but as soon as you looked away you forget all about them, plus there were another three of them hanging upside down from the rafters and sleeping like bats; a Judoon, a species of efficient and brutal rhinoceros looking intergalactic mercenary policemen and on the end was a peaceful and subservient member of the Ood, which had tentacles for a mouth and communicated telepathically via the glowing translation sphere they held in their right hand.

"There's something odd about the Ood, Bert!"

"There's something odd about you, Hugo," I replied laughing along with Blodwyn.

Next up, were two versions of the crippled and deformed megalomaniac, Davros. The first had him housed in a white/gold coloured Dalek base unit with a customised large domed top, open at the front where just his head and shoulders were visible, in his role as Emperor of the Imperial Daleks during the Imperial-Renegade Dalek Civil War. The second was the classic version of Davros with his withered body seated in a black Dalek base unit which served as his life support system, and resembled the evil twin brother, if he had one, of Professor X, the mutant founder and leader of the X-Men. Hugo busied himself with taking lots of photos.

At the end of the row we turned left into a row of classic monsters and aliens, and walked slowly past the K-1 'living' metal robot, which was created to replace humans carrying out hazardous tasks; a bit like Victor Frankenstein's monster, the Morbius monster was fashioned from human and alien body parts from crashed spacecraft, and was created to house the rescued brain of the executed renegade Time Lord, Morbius; with four eyes and ears, the human-bat-boar like Tetrap acted as henchmen to the renegade Time Lady, The Rani; an orange, shape-shifting nodule covered Zygon; a huge furry Yeti of Himalayan folklore, but actually a robot controlled by a formless being, known as The Great Intelligence; a militaristic and ruthless but honourable Sontaran clone and on the end was a tall, armoured and reptilian looking Martian Ice Warrior.

"This is the actual costume worn by Bernard Bresslaw, best remembered for starring in the 'Carry On' films, as Varga in the 1967 Second Doctor story, 'The Ice Warriors," Blodwyn explained to us. "Most of the classic costumes date back to the late sixties and have been lovingly and painstakingly restored," added Blodwyn.

"Yes, they look brilliant," replied Hugo.

As we wandered around the hall, incidental music was played from all eras of the Doctor, but all of us could not pinpoint with any certainty, which particular Doctor they belonged to!

Further along was a transparent case which housed five early Cybermen heads followed by a row of classic and modern Cybermen, showing their evolution together with a bronze headed, furry Cybershade and on the end, was a Cyberman made of wood! "What's the story with wooden one," I asked.

"It was specially made as a one off, to infiltrate the town of Christmas without triggering its alarm system, that the normal metal suit would have activated," replied Blodwyn.

"Sneaky," I answered.

The First Doctor had originally come across the Cybermen on Earth's near twin planet Mondas, where in an act of self-preservation the humans had progressed into a race of cold and emotionless Cyborgs. The early Cybermen retained their human brains and hands, together with a few organs and were dressed in metallic suits with a bulky chest mounted ventilator unit.

With every new Doctor, they became sleeker and less human looking with the brain as the only remaining organ, the rest being replaced by plastic and steel.

In the modern series, in a parallel universe Earth, Cybermen are created from homeless humans in factories run by a global business empire. Much like the precious metal silver in the form of a silver bullet, could kill a werewolf, it was found that gold whether touched or ingested by the Cybermen, could kill them.

In the centre of the hall were the costumes of the monsters and aliens of the Twelfth Doctor's Series Eight, arranged around the Half-Face Man's hot air balloon made of human skin.

Next up was a Weeping Angel of a race as old as time itself, which resembled a serene looking human sized stone angel you would find in most graveyards. Whenever someone looked at them they covered their faces as if weeping but would then turn into evil frightful creatures that attack with fangs and claws when you blink, so that they can feed off the energy of their victims unlived days by sending them back in time.

Slipping through a Skaro shaped doorway, we walked slowly between two rows of Daleks. Of all the enemies the Doctor has battled, his greatest must surely be, the Daleks, which have been encountered by every Doctor except the Eighth Doctor. Created in 1963 by screenwriter Terry Nation, they first appeared in the 'The Daleks', the second story of the First Doctor.

The thousand year civil war on the planet Skaro between the Kaleds and Thals led to nuclear, biological and chemical weapons being used which caused both sides to suffer mutations. The badly mutated Kaleds were genetically modified by the brilliant but evil scientist, Davros, who in the process removed every emotion except hate and encased them in armoured shells, famously described as 'pepper pots' and named them Daleks, an anagram of Kaleds. On several occasions the Daleks have come very close to being annihilated but have always manage to return from the brink of extinction.

A variety of different colours were used to denote the Daleks hierarchy, faction and function, together with some specialised versions such as the Special Weapons Dalek, better known as the 'Gunner' Dalek of the Imperial Daleks which was armed with an energy cannon, and there was even one that looked like it was made of stone!

"I read somewhere that Verity Lambert was on a bus one day and overheard some boys saying 'Exterminate' and knew then she had a winner on her hands," I commented.

"I think I read that; also did you know that Leicester holds the world record for the gathering of the most amount of Daleks in one place?" Hugo added.

"Really! Blodwyn exclaimed.

"Yes, they amassed ninety-five at the National Space Centre in 2008, it was done to mark the forty-fifth anniversary of their first appearance in 1963 and was verified by the Guinness Book of World Records."

"Wow, I never knew that," Blodwyn replied astonished.

"Nor me," I said.

Further on was a fixed Bronze Dalek that had been cut vertically in half, leaving only the front half, so children could walk inside and operate the eye, arm and gun.

"There's a long standing joke that the Daleks would never completely dominate the universe because of their supposed inability to climb stairs, but in the Seventh Doctor twenty-fifth anniversary story 'Remembrance of the Daleks', a Dalek is actually seen ascending a flight stairs!"

"Pesky Daleks," declared Hugo, laughing as we came across the set recreation of the dying Davros's chamber from the Series 9 two-parter, The Magician's Apprentice'/'The Witch's Familiar', with the multitude of cables surrounding him providing life support from every Dalek.

Nearby were the costumes of the Paternoster Gang, a late Victorian era trio of detectives based in Paternoster Row in the City of London, that occasionally helped the Eleventh and Twelfth Doctors, and consisted of inter-species married couple, Madame Vastra a female Silurian warrior, and Jenny Flint a human maid, together with their Sontaran butler, Strax.

The spin-off *Torchwood* series had a section to itself, which was set against the Hub safe door and had costumes of Captain Jack Harkness, an immortal time travelling action hero, former conman, rogue time agent and leader of Torchwood Three in his signature blue-grey RAF greatcoat with group captain rank insignia and the rest of his team, plus lots of props and Captain Jack's desk which was covered in memorabilia, together with the red/gold Supreme Dalek that Captain Jack destroyed with a 'defabricator' device in the final Ninth Doctor story 'The Parting of the Ways'.

The saddest section of the whole exhibition in my opinion, was the one dedicated to Clara Oswald, a companion of the Eleventh and Twelfth Doctors. The central feature was a TARDIS and a section of paving decorated with a painted floral mural with a sketch of Clara in one of the door panels by the graffiti artist Rigsy to commemorate Clara's death. Either side of the TARDIS were costumes worn by Clara.

"How did she die?" I asked.

"In short, Clara tried to outsmart Me, the Mayor of a 'trap street', which was an alien refugee camp in the middle of London, when Clara took on a death sentence Me had put on Rigsy for a crime he didn't commit. Thinking that the death sentence could be rescinded, Clara died a painful death, by a Quantum Shade in the form of a raven, hence the memorial…or did she die?" Replied Blodwyn looking emotional.

Carrying on, we came to the recreation of the War Doctor's barn from the show's Fiftieth Anniversary story 'The Day of the Doctor', with his TARDIS, the open version of the most dangerous weapon in the universe; the Moment device with its big red button and the costume of the Moment's human interface in the guise of Rose Tyler. The War Doctor was retroactively created between the Eighth and Ninth Doctors and fought alongside the Time Lords in the 400 year old Last Great Time War against the Daleks.

"Are all the TARDIS's the same?" I asked.

"Yes, they're basically the same, but with subtle differences like the rooftop light, windows and the instructions on one of the door panels, among others," answered Blodwyn.

From the Fourth Doctor's Console Room with its upgraded control console, which made it completely different to the previous doctors, which had a timeless quality about it, we walked across to the section devoted to the Twelfth Doctor's Series 9, with the costumes of the monsters, creatures and aliens, with the huge teleportation glass chamber from the 'Heaven Sent' story as the centre piece.

Further on were the red and blue Osgood boxes from the UNIT maintained facility located below the Tower of London, known as the Black Archive, and were seen in the Series 9 story 'The Zygon Inversion'.

Looking like a set of space-age Swiss, army knives, was a collection of the multi-function sonic screwdrivers used by most of the doctors, housed in a transparent case, together with a sonic cane used by the Eleventh Doctor plus the keys to the TARDIS.

At the far end of the of the hall was a Mummy, who was only visible to its victims, who then had only sixty-six seconds to live, aboard the luxurious *Orient Express* space train.

Behind the Mummy was a semi-circle of mannequins dressed in the original screen worn costumes of eleven of the thirteen Doctors, the first two being replicas. I sidestepped along the row of Doctors stopping at each one to observe the details, with Hugo and Blodwyn following along.

Dressed in a black frock coat of the late Victorian era of Jack the Ripper, the First Doctor was portrayed as a frail, forgetful and cantankerous grandfather figure, but he could be ruthless when required to; the Second Doctor wore an oversized black frock coat with stovepipe hat and looked scruffy and childlike but was a schemer; the Earthbound Third Doctor was a man of action, authorative and technically minded, flamboyantly dressed in a black velvet smoking jacket and red-lined cape; tall, whimsical and brooding, the Fourth Doctor was a jelly baby dispensing adventurer dressed in a wide brimmed hat, brown frock coat and a ridiculously long scarf; youthful and sensitive yet fearless, the Fifth doctor wore a red-trimmed cream coloured frock coat over a cricket jumper; mercurial and arrogant but passionate, the Sixth Doctor was garishly dressed in a red plaid frock coat; the easy-going and curious spoon playing Seventh Doctor, wore an ivory safari jacket with a crimson paisley scarf with a matching tie and hatband on the upturned brim of his Panama hat.

"Enjoying yourself, Hugo," I said as he took photo after photo of the Doctors.

"I am, this is brilliant," he replied, lowering his mobile phone for a moment.

Wearing a New Year's Eve fancy dress costume of American Old West folk hero, gambler and lawman James Butler 'Wild Bill' Hickok, the eccentric and romantic Eighth Doctor only appeared in one TV film adventure but has enjoyed numerous adventures in other media; The War Doctor, in his 'lived in' dark brown leather coat worn with a waistcoat and scarf plus a bandolier which housed his sonic screwdriver, was a warrior with a sense of duty, but cranky and tired from fighting the Daleks.

The show's revival in 2005 brought the haunted, brusque and down to earth Ninth Doctor who spoke with a northern accent, and dispensed with the flamboyant clothing of his predecessors and wore a distressed black leather pea coat and dark trousers; youthful and energetic, the Tenth Doctor was a charismatic adventurer dressed in a brown faux suede duster coat over a blue pinstriped dark brown suit, worn with an array of different coloured sneakers; boyish, but world weary with a quick temper, the Eleventh Doctor had a fondness for bowties and hats especially fezzes, worn with a Harris tweed brown jacket with elbow patches and the thrill seeking Twelfth Doctor, who was spiky and pragmatic and wore a navy blue three quarter length Crombie overcoat with a white long collared shirt. "Every time I come here there's always something different."

"How often do you come B?" Hugo asked.

"Roughly about once a year or so, but this is my fifth visit and sadly my last," Blodwyn replied mournfully, pushing out her bottom lip.

"I'm sure another exhibition will open again soon, maybe not in Cardiff, probably London or in another city," Hugo said putting an arm around Blodwyn.

"I really do hope they find another home for the collection soon, but the exhibition belongs here in Cardiff, where it is produced and filmed!"

"Yeah, you're so right, B," I replied while Hugo nodded his head in agreement.

Like most exhibitions and museums the exit led through to the gift shop, which was just like a Forbidden Planet shop, but dedicated to *Doctor Who* merchandise. Hugo was like a kid in a sweetshop, scanning the shelves for items to add to his collection.

"This is the only official *Doctor Who* shop in the world, Rick."

"Yeah, I can imagine, its massive," I replied watching Hugo scurrying around the mega amount of merchandise. After a bit he headed for one of the tills, paid and re-joined Blodwyn and I with a large carrier bag.

"What did you buy?" I asked being nosy.

"I only bought the Tom Baker 'Shada' DVD and the Monopoly *Doctor Who* 50th Anniversary Collector's Edition."

"Nice, I've never seen Shada, but I liked Douglas Adams's other *Doctor Who* stories 'City of Death' and the 'The Pirate Planet'. I couldn't get into his *Hitchhikers Guide to the Galaxy* when it was shown on TV but loved his Dirk Gently novels and the BBC4 *Dirk Gently* and the BBC America *Dirk Gently's Holistic Detective Agency* TV series.

"Do you want to grab a coffee in the Blue Box Café or wait until we get to the shopping centre?" Enquired Blodwyn.

"How far are the shops?" Asked Hugo.

"From the car park where we parked this morning, it's only ten to fifteen minutes away depending on the traffic."

"What do you think. Bert?"

"Yeah, we'll get a coffee at the shopping centre."

"Okay, so what did you both think of the Doctor Who Experience?"

"It was truly epic, B, it was like the whole *Doctor Who* universe gathered together in one place."

"Rick?"

"Yeah, it was brilliant, thank you, B."

"Good, I'm glad you both enjoyed it."

We left the exhibition and walked back the way we had come to the Mermaid Quay carpark and Blodwyn drove the short distance into the centre of Cardiff, crossing and re-crossing the River Taff in the process, before parking up in the NCP Westgate Street carpark.

Chapter Ten

We walked to the St. David's Centre shopping centre and came into the Eastside food and drink court were there were many places to eat. We pondered over Pret a Manger, Ed's Easy Diner and Patisserie Valerie before settling for the Muffin Break. "What do you both want to drink?" Asked Hugo.
"Latte please," I replied.
"Yes, I'll have a latte as well thank you, Hugo," said Blodwyn.
"Any cakes?"
"Ooh, let me have a look," replied Blodwyn, as we both accompanied Hugo to the counter. Blodwyn, after much deliberation settled on a slice of red velvet cake, while I went for a piece of baked cheesecake. I had first come across baked cheesecake on the TV show *Come Dine With Me* which was an excellent programme made even better by the narration of Dave Lamb much like Harry Hill's narration of *You've been Framed*. I was keen to try it as I had never had the baked version before, just the normal cheesecake, of which the New York one was my favourite.
While Hugo ordered the coffees and cakes, Blodwyn and I sat down at a table, which was two black, square tables shoved together with chairs that had brown leather backs and blue plush seats or blue leather backs with brown plush seats.
After a few minutes Hugo set the tray down on the table and we all took our coffees and cakes, Hugo had plumped for a piece of carrot cake.
Blodwyn kept looking into my cup, which I thought was strange. I drank the last of my latte and showed her the inside, Blodwyn then showed me the inside of her cup which had a smiley face printed on the bottom.
"When I go into Leicester, I always go to Krispy Kreme as I really like their latte, but I always seem to get stuck behind someone who orders a twelve box of doughnuts and then has a

hard time picking twelve and takes absolutely ages to fill the box. I thought I was bad making up my mind being a Libra, but these take the biscuit!"

"Don't you mean doughnut, Bert?" Hugo said sniggering like Muttley.

"It's because they have too much choice, there are just loads of different flavoured ones, I have the same problem myself with the three box!" Blodwyn replied, indicating with her eyes to something behind me, so I turned around, and there stood a man staring at me.

He was tall and lean and wore glasses below a grey woollen bobble hat, his hands were jammed into the pockets of a grubby looking orange Hi-Viz jacket over which he had a black rucksack on his back with a spirit level sticking out the top. Worn blue jeans tucked into a pair of scuffed tan leather 'rigger' boots completed his outfit. "Hi," I said.

"Alright mate, haven't seen you for a while, how's it going?"

"Good thanks, and you?" I replied, going along with it to see where it was leading, as I hadn't a clue who this guy was at all!

"Yeah, not bad thanks, how's the missus?"

"I'm not married," I answered, startled by the question.

"Oh Sorry…oh…err…sorry, I thought you were my mate Geoff," the man replied. "You look just like him," he added, and then he quickly strode away. I turned back to the table and shook my head in astonishment.

"He should've gone to Spec Savers, Bert," said Hugo laughing.

"Yeah, what was he doing, B?"

"He came up behind you and put his finger to his mouth to indicate for me to keep quiet and just stood there behind you, waiting for you to turn around."

"Strange fellow," I said, shaking my head again. Have we entered the Twilight Zone or summat? I have never been to Cardiff in my life, and that's the second person to call me Geoff today! The only other places I've been to in Wales are Llangollen, Tenby and Aberystwyth!"

"Maybe you have a doppelganger, Bert, wondering around Cardiff. Maybe if I went to, say, Durham for instance, I may have a doppelganger there."

"I doubt it Hugo, there can only be one of you!"

"I'll take that as a twisted compliment, Bert, but I find it funny that doppelgangers never meet each other."

"Maybe they can't meet face-to-face, like time travellers from the present can't occupy the same space in time as their past or future selves, maybe it's the same for doppelgangers."

"Spare a thought for this Geoff guy, who probably gets people coming up to him thinking he's Rick," added Blodwyn laughing.

"*Doo doo doo doo, doo doo doo doo,*" said Hugo laughing.

"You're about to enter another dimension, a dimension not only of sight and sound, but of mind." Hugo added, mimicking Rod Serling, the creator of *The Twilight Zone* TV series.

"I'm beginning to think we're in Weird Wales," I replied shaking my head.

"The Pandora shop is just a bit further up on the left," Blodwyn said laughing.

"Thanks, B," replied Hugo.

We finished our drinks and cakes and followed Blodwyn to the Pandora shop. "I'll meet you both across the other side of the street when you've finished, I'm just going to nip around the corner to Wilko's to get some hamster fluff for my sister, Betrys, so there's no need to rush," said Blodwyn.

"What on earth is hamster fluff?" I queried.

"It's a type of bedding material for hamsters," answered Blodwyn.

"What's the hamster's name?" Hugo had to ask.

"Large Marge."

"Is your sister sure it's a hamster and not a guinea pig?" Replied Hugo laughing along with me.

"I hope she doesn't feed it after midnight," I added. Blodwyn chortled as she disappeared through the glazed double doors.

Hugo and I went into the Pandora shop, which was very bright, white and pink! "So, d'ya know what you're looking for, Hugo?" I asked.

"Yes, another charm for her bracelet," replied Hugo, looking at a tray full of charms in a glass case. "Has she got many?"

"Hmm, about five or six, Bert, but this will be the first one I've bought her." Hugo finally chose a teddy bear charm and paid the bespectacled shop assistant wearing a Pandora logoed black T-shirt, who gift wrapped it.

We left the Pandora shop with Hugo looking very pleased with himself and exited the shopping centre and crossed the bustling pedestrianised shopping street called The Hayes, where we could see Blodwyn was waiting for us with her large bag of hamster fluff.

Hugo and I walked on into the Royal Arcade, and slowly strolled along the independent gift, jewellers, photo, clothes and Welsh textiles shops until we came to a shop called the Cardiff Antiques Centre. In the window were lots of diecast model vehicles, medals and first day covers. Hugo's eyes were riveted on a large-scale Sun Star silver coloured Routemaster bus.

"Have you seen the name on this bus, Bert?"

"No," I replied bending down to get a better look. "Oh yeah, Silver Lady," I laughed. "But why's it painted silver and not the traditional red?"

"On the original bus it's not silver paint, Bert, it's bare metal and was a one-off experiment in the 1960's to save money; no paint equals less weight equals better fuel economy."

"Didn't catch on then?"

"Err no, Bert."

We went inside the shop and it was wall-to-wall militaria, jewellery, old British and foreign coins and banknotes. Upstairs on the walls were a lot of signed framed pictures of sports, film and TV personalities, film posters and other memorabilia.

Blodwyn's eyes were immediately drawn to a picture of Sylvester Stallone punching the air as Rocky Balboa at the top of the steps of the Philadelphia Museum of Art in the famous scene from the film *Rocky*. After a lot of haggling over the price with the shop manager, Blodwyn eventually bought it. "I want a picture of Chewbacca next."

"Hhhhrrrrrrrrraaaaaareeeeerrrrrrrrrrr." Growled Hugo imitating the Wookie's voice.

From the Royal Arcade, Blodwyn led us on a short walk to Castle Street and showed us the exterior of the mediaeval Cardiff Castle. As we peeped through the entrance of the massive outer stone walls we could see the original eleventh-century motte and bailey castle built by the Normans on top of an earlier Roman Fort.

Blodwyn asked me to take a photo of her using her phone as she posed beside Cardiff Castle. Photo taken, she took back her phone and posted the photo on Facebook with the caption 'What's wrong with this photo?' and then showed us both.

"What *is* wrong with the photo, B?" Asked Hugo, looking puzzled.

"Take another look at the photo," replied Blodwyn, handing the phone back to Hugo.

"Do you know, Bert?"

"Yeah," I replied. Hugo studied the photo and kept looking at Blodwyn, then smiled.

"Oh, I get it now, we're in Cardiff and you're wearing a Swansea shirt."

"Mr observant," I laughed.

"I thought it was something to do with the castle, Bert."

On the other side of the road from the castle there was a Forbidden Planet shop sandwiched between a Caffe Nero and the Historical Wales shop which, from the window display was full of Welsh gifts, novelties and souvenirs.

We crossed over and entered the Forbidden Planet. It was nowhere near as large as the one we had visited in London last year, but it was still packed to the rafters with sci-fi, fantasy, cult TV and films merchandise. After a while of looking at the merchandise downstairs I found myself alone and wandered upstairs to find Blodwyn looking at the *Game of Thrones* stuff, while Hugo was looking at the *Doctor Who* and *Star Wars* stuff.

"It's Bu's birthday next week, and she loves…well we both love *Game of Thrones*," said Blodwyn, kneeling down looking through a row of mugs. She finally settled on one with the head of a grey wolf on it while Hugo found a *Doctor Who* electronic QLA Anti-time device. "What's that then Hugo," I asked.

"It's some sort of Dalek/Cyberman hybrid weapon that sends their enemies into the Time Vortex."

"Nasty," I replied laughing, as we all made our way downstairs where Blodwyn and Hugo paid for their items.

"Hi B," said a man with a boyish smile as we stepped out of the shop.

"Oh, hi Hammy", replied B with a smile. Hammy was short and squat and looked like a forty-something year old student, and had bushy black hair sticking out of a plain black baseball cap and had one of those weirdy beardy things going on with no moustache that made him look as if he was a member of one of those groups that shunned modern technology like electricity, and if he had grown it to hide his chin, he had failed miserably as it was unbelievably bigger than Bruce Campbell's, who had starred in the *Evil Dead* and *Army of Darkness* films and was known in the industry as 'The Chin'.

He wore a red T-shirt with a black fire breathing dragon in the centre together with a pair of three-quarter length beige shorts worn with black trainers and ankle socks, a black rucksack hung heavily down his back and he was carrying a 'Game' logoed plastic bag. An expensive looking pair of headphones hung around his neck together with an identity card in a plastic holder suspended from a blue cord.

"Hammy and I were in the same class at school." Blodwyn told us. "These are my friends Rick and Hugo." We all said hi to one another.

"How's your Mum?" Asked Hammy.

"Yes, she's good thanks, and yours?"

"Same as usual." A faint smile crossed Blodwyn's face.

"Well I must get on, nice to see you again B, and meet your friends, remember me to you Mum."

"I will, Hammy." We all said goodbye as Hammy sauntered off.

"He's alright to talk to but has the personality of a c…"

"Cheese sandwich?" I proffered.

"I was going to say crayon, Rick!"

"A crayon, I like it," said Hugo, letting out a guffaw.

"I took him to the Birmingham Comic Con a few years ago and on the way back, I dropped him off outside his house and his Mother came out and told me that *my* Mother must be waiting for me back home with a casserole!"

"Bit random," I replied.

"Yes, I don't think she liked me much."

"Beam me up Snotty," Hugo added.

"Exactly," replied Blodwyn smiling.

"What's his proper name?"

"You know... I have absolutely no idea, Rick, everyone just called him Hammy."

"Jolly dee."

"We'd better head back home if you're sure about going to Black Woods this evening," Blodwyn said.

"Yeah, I'm looking forward to it already," I answered unconvincingly.

"Trust me, it will be a blast, Bert," Hugo replied clapping his hand on my back. "Do you want to come with us, B?"

"Thanks, but no thanks, Hugo, I've had more than my fill of the great outdoors when I was in the RAF. I'll have a long soak in the bath with some wine then watch a bit of tele and then read some more of my book before going to sleep in *my* warm, comfy bed."

"Looks look it's just you and me then, Bert."

"Yeah, I was afraid of that."

"It'll be an adventure, Bert, all that fresh air and being at one with nature."

"You'd make a useless salesman, Hugo."

Chapter Eleven

We arrived back at Blodwyn's, stowed away our stuff and had a cup of tea. "Right then," said Blodwyn. "You're going to need some supplies," and then disappeared into what looked like a box room.

A few minutes later she reappeared carrying two nylon carrying bags, and a rucksack. On one of the tube like carrying bags, Blodwyn depressed the toggle on the red cord at the top, opening up the neck and peeled the bag down over the foldable chair inside rather like peeling off a silk stocking and then set it down on the kitchen floor upright and unfolded it. The chair had a polyester seat, back and arms over a metal frame with a cup holder in the right arm, which looked like the type people took to festivals and air shows and could also be used for fishing and camping. Hugo immediately sat down on it to test it out. "Very comfy," he commented.

"Yes, it's better than sitting on the cold ground," replied Blodwyn. Hugo jumped out of the chair and I sat in it. "Yes, it's just the job, B."

From inside the rucksack, Blodwyn pulled out a set of mess tins which were stacked one inside the other, two olive green plastic mugs and two torches. The first torch was a military type green plastic one with an angled head and a clip for attaching to a belt or strap. I checked the torch worked. The second was a large, plastic and rubber AA heavy duty LED torch with an in-built carrying handle in yellow and black, which I also checked worked. "D'ya have any spare batteries B?" Blodwyn pulled out some packs of batteries from the bottom of the rucksack and then placed them back inside. "You can take this rucksack with you Rick, as you only brought a holdall with you.

"Thanks," I replied.

"Have you got any NVG's?" Asked Hugo.

"NVG's?" questioned Blodwyn. "No, but I have something just as good," Blodwyn replied winking at me, and returned to the box room and came back with what looked like an aircrew head torch. "This head torch will help you with your night vision Hugo." The head torch had elasticated straps that fitted around and over the centre of the head. "I use it when I go running either early in the morning or late evening." Hugo pulled it over his head and Blodwyn adjusted the straps and talked him through the different light modes.

"You can buy beanie hats now with an in-built light," I said.

"Where from, Bert?"

"From those gadget shop places they have in the Highcross Centre, though no doubt you can also buy them off the internet."

"Cheers, Bert, I'll have a look when I next go into Leicester."

Blodwyn opened up the head height cupboards and sifted through the contents. On the right she kept the pickles, sauces and condiments and pulled out a jar of piccalilli and put it on the dining table. Then she rummaged through the left-hand side which contained the tinned goods and removed a tin of Bacon Grill. "I don't know where this came from?" Blodwyn said, placing it on the table. "It must be Bu's, but she won't mind."

Opening up the next cupboard, Blodwyn reached for a box of Oat So Simple Golden Syrup porridge and opening it up, removed six sachets. 'I've got no soup, but you can take these porridge sachets which will make you a hot meal, or there are some tins of beans, beef ravioli and mackerel in curry sauce."

"We'll take the porridge thanks, B," I replied turning my nose up at the canned goods on offer. Blodwyn tucked the sachets of porridge together with two KitKat bars and some sachets of sugar for Hugo into the mess tins. From the top shelf of the fridge door, Blodwyn removed a tub of margarine and a pack of mild cheddar cheese slices, and from the lower shelf a two pint plastic bottle of milk. "Make yourself some sandwiches with the Bacon Grill and cheese, the cutlery is in the drawer under the drainer."

"Have you got any bananas, B?" Hugo asked.

"No sorry, I ate the last one this morning."

"That's okay, I do though love a banana and brown sauce sandwich." Blodwyn and I immediately stopped what we were doing and looked at Hugo strangely while shaking our heads. "What!" said Hugo, "They're lovely."

"Even if I had some bananas, I've got no brown sauce as I'm a ketchup person," replied Blodwyn laughing.

"Bacon grill and cheese it is then," Hugo grinned.

Don't get me wrong, I love Bacon Grill, but I always found it was a bit of a mission trying to remove it from the tin. It had a ring pull on the top to pull off the lid, but then I had to use a tin opener to open up the bottom and then push the bottom through the tin to expel the meat onto a plate. After using this method, I sliced it up while Hugo buttered eight slices of bread.

"How d'ya want your sandwiches Hugo?"

"I'll have the Bacon Grill with cheese and some piccalilli thanks, Bert."

"Okay, I'll have the same." I put two slices of the Bacon Grill together with a cheese slice on four slices of buttered bread followed by a dollop of piccalilli and topped them with the other four slices of buttered bread and cut them horizontally.

"I wanted mine cut diagonally," said Hugo with a grin as he passed me two pieces of tinfoil he had torn off from the roll, and I wrapped up half the sandwiches in each.

Out of another cupboard, Blodwyn pulled out a large matt black Thermos vacuum flask with a carrying handle and a stainless-steel cup. "The flask has a twist and pour top so you don't have to remove the top to pour the coffee and will keep the contents hot or cold for twenty-four hours."

"When you put hot water in a flask, it keeps it hot, and when you put cold water in, it keeps it cold, how does the flask know the difference?" Blodwyn and I stared at Hugo in astonishment, but he was already laughing.

Blodwyn filled the kettle to its capacity and flipped the switch for it to boil.

"Do you want the milk in the flask or separate?" Asked Blodwyn.

"In the flask please," I replied. Blodwyn opened the jar of Kenco coffee beside the kettle and put four heaped teaspoons into the flask and then added a generous amount of milk and then had to wait a minute for the kettle to boil before pouring the boiling water into the flask and securing the top. 'Can one of you grab a toilet roll from the bathroom?' Blodwyn asked.

"There's no way I'm having a number two in the woods in the dark!" Hugo exclaimed as I returned with the toilet roll.

"If you need to go Hugo, you need to go," I said with a smirk. "And it's two-ply so it's nice and soft for your sensitive arse."

"I didn't mean for you to wipe your bottom on it, but to wipe your hands or clean your mess tins or whatever, and then you can dispose of it on the fire, but as Rick says if you need to go you need to go, Hugo, unless you prefer to use leaves or grass!"

"I'll go before we leave," replied Hugo.

Blodwyn's final items for us to take was an old copy of the *South Wales Star* and a green plastic lighter, of the sort you could buy five for a pound. I looked at the amount of stuff piled up on the dining table. "We're only going to the woods for one night, not an expedition along the Amazon!"

"It's better to take too much than too little," replied Blodwyn. "You don't want to get cold and hungry in the woods, because that will make you miserable, and if you feel miserable you will want to give up and come back here, and you don't want to do that, do you?"

"Okay. Okay," I said raising my hands in surrender. "No, we don't, B."

"Good, and make sure your mobiles are fully charged before its time to go, and you'd better take this bin bag with you as it may be a bit of a mess there with bottles, cans and other assorted rubbish."

"Yeah, we will," I replied taking the bin bag as Hugo and I divvied up the items on the table and stowed them away in our rucksacks and I added my Fujifilm Finepix S2960 camera on the top of mine and with some difficulty zipped it up.

"May I suggest you have something substantial to eat before you go on your monster hunt," said Blodwyn.

"I was gonna suggest that, Bert," Hugo added.

"What did you have in mind, B?" I said. Blodwyn removed a leaflet attached to the fridge door by a TARDIS shaped fridge magnet. "These do very good meals," Blodwyn replied, handing me the leaflet. Hugo and I sat down at the kitchen table and perused the 'Bay Xpress' door-to-door delivery and takeaway leaflet. It was full of pizzas, burgers and chicken meals together with specials like home-made faggots, sausages, lasagne and curries served with, depending on the meal, rice, chips, salad, garlic bread, beans and peas. "I think I'll have the Trio of Sausages," I said, which came with chips and peas or beans. "With beans."

"Hugo?"

"Erm... I'll have the...err...Local Faggots." I looked at the menu and it consisted of two faggots, chips peas and onion gravy. "What are you having B?"

"I'm going to have the Vegetable Lasagne," she replied without looking at the menu, which came with chips, house salad and garlic bread, I read. I handed Blodwyn back the menu and she phoned them up and placed our order.

"Has somebody changed the toilet roll around? I changed the roll this morning before we went out and I'm sure the loose end was at the front."

"That was me," replied Blodwyn. "I always have the loose end at the rear, I'm afraid."

"It's no big deal B, I just thought I was going mad that's all," replied Hugo laughing.

The meals order came after about half an hour and we all heartily tucked into our food and after a final cup of tea we were ready to leave for our night in the woods.

Chapter Twelve

Leaving Blodwyn's house, we stowed our rucksacks in the boot and Blodwyn drove the Opel for about twenty minutes before she came to a stop in the middle of a street with a pathway which ran between a row of houses.

"If you follow the path you will come to a metal kissing gate on the right, go through that and you're in Black Woods, follow the trail past the pond on the right and then you will come to a clearing. Give me a call no matter what the time, that you want to be picked up from here."

"Thanks B," I said as Hugo and I got out of the car and removed our rucksacks from the boot. "See you tomorrow," I said as Hugo and I waved to Blodwyn.

"Have fun," replied Blodwyn with a snicker and gave a short toot on her horn as she accelerated away. We watched until she had vanished from sight.

I looked at my mobile phone for the time, which read 18:27. *We're about to spend the next twelve hours or so in these woods,* I thought as I looked up at the sky, which was topaz coloured with lazy white cotton wool clouds which had grey undersides that skimmed across the horizon. Behind me there loomed a huge graphite coloured cloud, shaped like some fantastical rocket ship from a 1950's sci-fi film, silently on route to Mars or beyond.

I removed my camera from my rucksack and slung it around my neck, while Hugo dug out a pair of cheap looking binoculars and hung them around his neck and his 'Deputy Dawg' style winter cap and put it on his bald head, fastening the ear flaps up over the crown. We heaved the rucksacks onto our backs and proceeded to walk along the heavily cracked path, which was a patchwork of old and new tarmac bordered on both sides by weeds.

On the left was a six-foot high metal fence with nasty looking three-pronged spikes on the top, which had signboards at intervals along it saying 'Warning Dragon Security' with an 0800 number interspersed with 'CCTV In Operation' one of which had the name 'Shaz' spray painted across it, protecting what looked like a factory unit. On the right were hedges, bushes and brambles, behind which were traditional featheredge wooden fencing, some with lattice frames at the top, which marked the boundary of the back gardens of a row of semi-detached houses.

"Switch your phone from ring to vibrate, we don't want our phones ringing in the woods," I said as I switched over my phone. "Okay, Bert."

After a bit the houses fell away and were replaced by low wooden post and rail fencing, some of which were broken or had missing rails, and we could've easily nipped in through a gap in the bushes to enter the woods, but we continued along the path towards the kissing gate as Blodwyn had told us to.

As we walked on, we came across a mouldy looking mattress and broken white furniture that had obviously been dumped there, and further on, a supermarket shopping trolley lay abandoned on its side, together with a traffic cone. "It's amazing how traffic cones just randomly appear," Hugo said nonplussed.

"Yeah, in an episode of *Red Dwarf* Lister is baffled when he wakes after a night of partying to find one in his bed, three million years into deep space!"

We carried on, and what I first thought was a discarded portable TV, turned out to be on closer inspection to have a steel tubular base with black plastic footplates, and from the label on the front, was a Lateral Thigh Trainer. "Looks like it's a popular fly tipping area, Bert."

"Yeah, looks that way," I replied as we passed some more unwanted household junk and a rolled-up carpet. "Shall we take it with us, Bert?" Hugo asked unfurling the faded pink carpet slightly. "It might be useful to lay on the ground and put our seats on top of it."

"Good idea but no, leave it, you don't know how long it's been there and besides it's probably got its own little eco system going on inside it."

"Yuck," replied Hugo pulling a face as he cast away the carpet sharpish.

The bushes to our right unexpectedly started to rustle and we came to an abrupt halt and listened intently. "There's definitely something prowling about in those bushes."

"Might be a fox, Bert." Then suddenly a cat appeared, making us both start. "Bloody hell," said Hugo with his hand on his heart.

"I hope you're not gonna be like this all night Hugo?"

"Like what, Bert?"

"Jittery."

"I'll be alright, it just gave me a start that's all." The cat had grey fur with black stripes, and a white underbelly, front feet and hind legs and feet, plus the most amazing sea-green eyes. Hugo immediately went down on one knee and called "Here puss, puss, puss". The cat meowed softly and padded over to Hugo, and after stroking its head, he picked it up.

"Well that was easy Bert, we can go home now, case solved!"

"What! You really think that cat is the Beast of Black Woods?" I said with mock incredulity. "It's not exactly the six-legged hairy summat with goggly eyes summat or other you said we were after, is it?"

"Do you mean the winged seven-foot, six legged furry lizard with blood stained tusks and horns?"

"That's what I said, Hugo."

"It was worth a try, Bert." Hugo replied smirking. "Can you take a photo of us?" I shook my head and took a photo with my camera and showed it to Hugo, who smiled and nodded his approval of the pic. "C'mon, put the cat down and let's carry on." Hugo released the cat which quickly returned to the bushes.

We walked on a bit more and finally came upon the kissing gate although the path carried on past it. I undid the latch and pushed the gate forward and walked through into a semi-circular enclosure, and then had to close the gate behind me to allow entry into Black Woods. Hugo did the same and the gate closed behind him with a clang, disturbing some pigeons in the trees, which flew away, beating their wings noisily, which sounded as if they were clapping. Foraging squirrels scampered away from us across the leaf strewn woodland floor as we took our first steps into the forbidding Black Woods. "This is it Bert," Hugo said surveying the wood. "The truth is in Black Woods!"

"I hope so," I replied as we trekked along the dusty well-trodden narrow trail, which went downhill for a while before sweeping around to the left and ran like a brown coloured ribbon, through the trees. Both sides of the trail were littered with discarded beer cans and cigarette packets. Piled up logs and tree trunks lay everywhere, like sleeping giants on a bed of leaves, covered over like a blanket by the undergrowth, which was slowly assimilating them. The predominantly light, mid and dark green hues of the woods were broken up by large swathes of yellow from dandelions mixed together with the white of daisies and every now and again by violet-blue pockets of bluebells.

Hugo gave out a yelp and quickly recoiled his left hand.

"What's wrong, Hugo?"

"Stinging nettles."

"Let me have a look." Hugo showed me his hand which had reddened and was covered in a rash of whitish pimples. "Pour some water on it while I look around for a dock plant." Sure enough, growing in between the nettles there were plenty of them. I bent down and plucked a few of the broad, green dock leaves and crushed them up in my hand then squeezed the juice out onto Hugo's hand, as he rubbed it on the affected area.

"Cheers Bert."

"It's the same when you drink nettle wine."

"How do you mean, Bert?"

"Because, you have to drink dock leaf wine afterwards," I said trying to look serious.

"Really!" Said Hugo looking amazed.

"Gotcha!" I replied, then curled the index finger of my right hand into a hook shape and inserted it into the right corner of my mouth and yanked on it a few times like a fish that had been hooked.

"Don't worry Bert, I shall get you back," Hugo said smiling.

"I'm still waiting from the last time I got you."

"You know what they say about revenge, Bert, don't you?"

"Dig two graves?"

"Isn't that a line from a Bond film?"

"Yeah, *For Your Eyes Only*, the beautiful half Greek, half British Melina Havelock has killed the Cuban hitman who murdered her parents, and now wants to take revenge on the guy she saw paying the hitman. Bond tells her 'The Chinese have a saying, before setting out on revenge, you first dig two graves.'"

"Isn't that the one with the 2CV?"

"Yeah."

"Well, *my* revenge will be served like gazpacho soup, Bert…cold!"

"Jolly dee," I replied smiling.

A man walking his dog was approaching us. The dog, a black Labrador was off his lead and came bounding enthusiastically towards us. "It's okay guys, he's just being friendly," the man called out. The man was dressed in a what looked like a green alpine hat with a spray of feathers tucked into the left-side of a darker green coloured, corded hatband and a grey fleece with white woollen trim on the collar, cuffs and pockets together with blue jeans. A grey 'Van Dyke' style moustache and beard rather like Oliver Reed's 'Athos' character in *The Return of the Musketeers* film, gave him a distinguished look.

"Hello boy," said Hugo as he bent down on one knee and greeted the Labrador with repeated stokes of his head and neck. "What's his name?" Hugo asked, looking up at the man.

"Muldoon," the man replied.

"Hello Muldoon," said Hugo. I stood there looking at the Labrador, who had large friendly eyes and was clearly excited and wagging his tail.

Chapter Thirteen

As we ventured deeper into the heart of the woods, it began to look more primitive like 'the land that time forgot' and any minute now I was convinced we would come across Doug McClure being chased by a dinosaur. The treetops leaned inwards, forming a leafy canopy, blocking out the sun which made the woods appear noticeably darker. Hugo sat down on one of the sawn up tree trunks, took off his rucksack and reached into the netting pocket for his bottle of water. "It looks a bit like an enchanted forest," Hugo said looking around him.

"Yeah, well you'd better keep your eye out for the woodcutter," I replied as I sat beside Hugo on the tree trunk but kept my rucksack on as Hugo smiled and took a swig from the bottle as we both listened as the woods were alive with the constant chatter of probably hundreds of unseen birds nestling in the trees. I watched as two blackbirds and a magpie were skipping about and bobbing their heads as they pecked at the ground, totally oblivious to our presence. Hugo raised his open palm to his temple in a military style salute. "I salute you Mr Magpie."

"What's that all about?" I enquired.

"It's to prevent sorrow for seeing a single magpie, as in the nursery rhyme, Bert."

"Yeah, I've heard the rhyme from the *Magpie* TV show," I said shaking my head.

"I enjoyed that show, Bert; it was like a trendier version of *Blue Peter*."

"Me too," I answered. Thirst slaked, Hugo offered me the bottle and I wiped the top and took a quick gulp and passed it back. "Thanks," I said, as I got to my feet. Hugo returned the bottle to its pocket, heaved the rucksack onto his back and we continued our trek along the trail with twigs crunching and breaking with a snap underfoot.

On our right we passed the roughly circular placid pond which Blodwyn had told us about, that had a rusting shopping trolley in the centre with various insects darting and skimming across the surface of the water. Five flat topped huge boulders were dotted around it.

A light breeze whispered through the woods, causing the trees to creak, the branches to bend and the leaves to rustle.

"You don't think there's bats in these woods do you, Bert? Hugo said looking up at the trees. "What, you think there's a flock of vampire bats up there waiting to swoop down and suck us both dry of blood?"

"Well, if there are vampire bats up there, they've travelled a long way from Central and South America, Bert, and it's not a flock it's a colony of bats."

"Are you some kind of bat expert now, after dressing like one?"

"No," Hugo laughed. "Didn't you learn as a kid the group names of animals?"

"Yeah, like a flock of sheep or a herd of cows."

"Hmm, well a group of bats is called a colony."

"What's the group name for squirrels?"

"Dray or scurry."

"Well Hugo, it's more likely to be a dray or scurry of squirrels in the trees rather than bats."

We eventually emerged from the woods into a sun lit, large kidney-shaped lush glade which had a tall grassy bank that ran like a wall along its outer edge. In the middle of the glade we found the patch of blackened earth which Blodwyn had told us about, where people lit campfires. Hugo and I both removed our rucksacks and laid them on the ground.

As Blodwyn had warned us, the area was covered with beer and energy drink cans, spirit bottles, hundreds of cigarette ends and fast food cartons. "I think the first thing we should do, is to gather as much twigs and wood as we can before it gets too dark and then try and pick up most of the rubbish using the bin bag."

"If we empty our rucksacks, Bert, we can use them to put the wood in."

"That's a good idea, Hugo," I replied. I removed the camera from around my neck and took my jacket off and Hugo did the same with his coat, hat and binoculars as it was still quite warm. We then emptied all of our gear out of the rucksacks and walked over to the tree line and began to pick up all the fallen twigs and branches at the base of the trees and in between them and pile them into the rucksacks. We did this a couple of times and at the end had quite a sizeable amount of wood piled up. I found an empty plastic bag among the stuff we had removed from our rucksacks and scrabbling around on the ground, picked up handfuls of the brown, crisp leaves, which looked as if they had been toasted, and stuffed them into the bag.

I rooted out the newspaper from amongst the stuff scattered on the ground and scrunched up the double pages into loosely packed balls and also added some of the toilet paper, building them up into a nest in the centre of the scorched earth and then sprinkled the leaves over them. Hugo then passed me the thinnest twigs first, and I steepled them around the paper and leaves then he passed me progressively thicker and larger pieces of wood which I carefully placed around the twigs. I had purposefully left a small gap in the wood facing the wind, which hopefully, would help to fan the flames. I found the lighter from the pile of stuff lying around and set fire to a rolled-up piece of newspaper and poked it through the gap I had left. I learnt the art of making fires as a teenager on the large field in front of my parents' house.

"Man...fire," Hugo chanted looking up to the sky, while beating his chest repeatedly. I too looked up to the sky but for completely different reasons.

After we had finally got the fire started, Hugo and I began to pick up the rubbish that had been left around where we were going to spend the night and put it into the bin bag Blodwyn had provided. There were quite a few McDonald's paper cups mostly for cold drinks with only a few coffee cups, which I checked each one to see if the 'bean' sticker had been removed and managed to find one that hadn't. I went over to my jacket and pulled my wallet out and went through all the other loyalty cards I had for a free coffee until I came to the McDonald's one and peeling the sticker off the cup stuck it on my card with the other three which meant I only now needed another two for a free coffee. "Have you come across any McDonald's coffee cups, Hugo?"

"A few, I've been keeping my eye out for the stickers for you, but they've all been removed, Bert."

"Thanks," I replied stuffing my wallet into my right-hand trouser pocket, then returned to picking up the rest of the rubbish but I drew the line at the fag ends, it wasn't because I disliked smokers, it was the filthy fag ends and full ashtrays I had a problem with.

As a child I used to love going to Molly's corner shop to buy a packet of 'Mounties' sweet cigarettes, on the back of which were pictures of the various activities of the Mounties. I used to swagger about acting like 'Charlie Big Potatoes,' puffing away on my 'cigarettes' which were coloured red on one end and trying to flip them up and catch them in my mouth the right way round with the red tip facing out or have the cigarette dangle from my bottom lip and talk in an American accent. But they never led me to buying real cigarettes as most of my siblings and friends had done.

With the fire blazing away nicely, Hugo and I gathered together the stuff we had emptied from our rucksacks and filled them again and then untied the chair carrying bags from our rucksacks, and removed the chairs from the bags, unfolded them and placed them with their backs near the grassy bank and we both flopped down in them.

"This is the life ay, Bert," said Hugo with his hands behind his head and his feet spread out. "All's we have to do now is wait."

"Yeah, I've always wanted to spend the night in a wood, sitting on a camp chair instead of being tucked up in a nice warm bed." I had never enjoyed camping, when I was about fourteen or fifteen I had gone camping with three friends to Llangollen; there was always grass in the food, the farm shop to stock up on milk, bread and other sundries was miles away and I never knew how much water weighed until I had to lug a container of it from the filling point back to the tent.

"Think of it as character building, Bert."

"Hmm," was all I could say, faced with the prospect of the long night ahead was not my idea of fun. "Coffee?"

"Yes please, Bert, NATO Standard!" I shook my head as I removed the flask from my rucksack and poured out the steaming hot coffee into the mugs Hugo was holding out, and put the flask on the ground next to my chair and then reached into my rucksack again and removed all of the sugar sachets from the mess tins and handed them to Hugo. "Cheers, Bert," Hugo replied placing my mug on the ground next to the flask and added the contents of two of the sugar sachets to his drink. I picked up my mug and sat back in my chair, sipping the hot coffee.

I looked at my mobile phone, it was 19:47, and watched the sun indirectly as it reluctantly disappeared below the horizon and the woods were transformed into a more brooding place by the soft, half-light, half-darkness realm of twilight, between sunset and dusk and it suddenly brought a chill to the air despite the roaring fire. I found my jacket and put it on.

The gradually darkening sky gave it a very pale blue look and what clouds remained had a violet tint to them and caused the once vibrant colours of the wood to slowly start to fade to a sad sepia tone. Squadrons of chirping birds flew overhead in a loose formation followed by a few stragglers bringing up the rear

I fished out my wallet from my trouser pocket and took out the clear plastic container that contained a SD card and then pulling my rucksack closer removed my camera. Turning the camera upside down, I opened up the battery compartment, inserted the card into the slot and then closed the cover and then looped the carrying strap around my neck.

The fire hissed and crackled as I put on some more wood and it gave off a surprising amount of heat. "What's the stick for Hugo?"

"It's a not a stick it's a club, Bert," Hugo said of his yard-longish branch, with a large, gnarled knot on the thick end. "It's there just in case we get attacked by some large slavering beast, or failing that, I can use some of my Feng Shui skills on it."

"And just how exactly does arranging your furniture in harmony and balance help you to fight off *this* slavering beast, Hugo?"
"Did I say Feng Shui?"
"Yeah, you know you did."
"Sorry, I meant Ju Jitsu," Hugo replied laughing.
"Do you know Ju Jitsu, or any other martial arts?"
"I've watched *Enter the Dragon* several times, Bert!"
"You'd better stick to the arts your familiar with."
"Like what?"
"Like those involving paper."
"I'll have you know, Bert, Ruth loves my origami swans."
"What woman wouldn't, Hugo?"

Chapter Fourteen

"I wish we'd have brought some marshmallows with us," said Hugo, attaching the head torch to the front of his cap.

"What for?"

"To toast."

"Thank gawd for that, I thought you were gonna say to play Chubby Bunny with, then!"

"What's Chubby Bunny?"

"D'ya remember that woman I told you about on the coach that went to her niece's birthday party and took her own food with her because she was on a diet?"

"Yes, Bert, what was her name?"

"What?"

"You referred to her as that woman, what's her name?"

"Oh right, it's Audrey, Audrey Sinclair. Well, anyway, I was invited to *Audrey's* fiftieth birthday party, and amongst the various party games, there was one called Chubby Bunny, which I had never heard of myself before then. It involves people sat round taking turns to stuff marshmallows in their mouths without swallowing, while clearly saying the words Chubby Bunny. The winner is the one who can stuff the most amount in their mouth, and then clearly say Chubby Bunny."

"How many did *you* manage, Bert?"

"I didn't play the silly game! D'ya wanna KitKat?"

"Save it for me, I'll have it later."

"Jolly dee," I replied tucking into my KitKat and putting Hugo's into my jacket pocket.

"You know there are still people who believe that the Moon landings were faked."

"Yes, I could believe their concerns if there was only one Moon landing, Bert, but there were six! Are they going to say that *all* six were faked?"

"I loved watching the news when the Apollo Program was covered by Peter Fairley, the ITN Science Editor, and I would buy any newspapers and magazines that had news and pictures of it. In fact, I still have a copy of the *Daily Mirror* from 21 July 1969. Anyway, I recently watched an episode of the *MythBusters* TV series which recreated some of the claims that the conspiracy theorists said were faked about the Moon landing, and they busted every one of them!"

"I haven't seen that episode, Bert."

"I watched it on YouTube in the library. One of the claims was that when the astronauts planted the US flag on the Moon, it flapped about as if there was a breeze from somewhere. The *MythBusters* Team built a replica assembly that held the US flag so it would not droop when planted on the Moon. First, they tried it out in normal conditions and when they planted it, the flag began to flap. In a research centre vacuum chamber, to create the zero atmosphere conditions on the Moon, they acted out planting the flag again, and it also began to flap. It was found that the momentum caused by the actual act of planting the flag on the Moon's surface caused it to flap about and not a breeze. Another conspiracy theory that they busted in the vacuum chamber was a photo of Aldrin's boot print on the Moon's surface which was really sharp and according to the doubters could not have been made in the vacuum of space. The team first tested if dry or wet sand made a more distinguishable print by making a footprint in both wearing an astronaut boot, naturally the wet sand made a clearer impression than the dry. In the vacuum chamber they placed soil similar in composition to that found on the Moon and then stepped on it using the astronaut boot, which made a clear boot print. Then, there was the claim that a photo taken by Neil Armstrong of Buzz Aldrin descending the ladder of the lunar module with the sun behind it must have been faked, as he is shown to be clearly visible against the black shadow of the module, so the conspiracists claim there must have been another light source other than the sun, like a studio light. To test this, the team created a portion of the Moon's surface and an *Eagle* Lunar Module together with an action figure of an astronaut, all in one sixth scale. Also, the material they used to simulate the Moon's surface had a similar colour and light reflection. They then took a photo which matched Armstrong's original and the toy astronaut was clearly visible because of the Sun's rays reflecting off the surface of the Moon to illuminate Aldrin."

"Do you think Buzz was pre-destined to go to the Moon, Bert, as his mother's maiden name was Moon?"

"I wouldn't have thought so, but it's an interesting theory."

"What about Sara Blizzard then?"

"The BBC weather presenter? I have no idea if her surname led her into being a weather presenter, but it's a pretty apt name," I replied yawning, while looking at the time on my phone, which read 21:03.

"Wasn't there was a film about a fake Moon landing, Bert?"

"Yeah, *Capricorn One*, but it wasn't the Moon, it was a fake landing on Mars. On the first manned mission to Mars, just minutes before take-off the hatch of the capsule is opened, and the three astronauts are asked to leave and then whisked away by jet to an abandoned military base in the desert where they are told that the cut-price life support system in the capsule doesn't work and the crew would have died three weeks into the mission. Anyway, the crewless rocket takes off on schedule and the crew are then taken into what looks like a film studio where a replica surface of Mars has been created, together with a Mars landing module and they are coerced through threats to their families into acting out leaving the module and stepping down onto the Martian surface and planting the US flag, the film of which will be seen back on Earth. On the journey 'home' the crew talk to their wives from inside the capsule and the commander tells his wife about a holiday they had enjoyed in Yosemite, and she is shown looking rather puzzled. The crew then board the jet at the abandoned base to be placed in a space capsule that will be set adrift in the Pacific Ocean like they have splashed down, to await recovery. On the journey back to Earth however, an alert signal on a console at mission control shows that the heat shield has separated from the capsule and it has disintegrated on re-entry into the Earth's atmosphere, killing the crew. This info is passed to the jet and it returns to the base. The crew figure out something has gone wrong with the mission and escape from the base in the jet, but it's low on fuel and they are forced to crash land in the desert and decide to split up and walk off in different directions. Two of the crew are quickly caught by helicopters and are killed off camera, leaving only the commander left. An ambitious reporter sees the film footage of the commander's wife looking puzzled when he mentions going to Yosemite and goes to see her, where she explains that they didn't go to Yosemite at all but went to an Old West type town where a movie was being filmed. Her husband had become fascinated with how it was made and had commented that with such technology you could convince people that something so fake could look so real. Another reporter tells the reporter the location of the abandoned military base and he travels there and finds evidence of the astronauts presence there. He then hires the pilot of a crop spraying aircraft which is piloted by Telly Savalas from *Kojak*..."

"Hey Crocker, who loves ya baby!" Hugo interjected, imitating Kojak.

"Hmm, anyway they search the desert in the aircraft, and find the commander at an abandoned petrol station being attacked by the helicopters. The aircraft lands and the commander jumps onto the wing, and they are then pursued by the helicopters which are blinded when they are doused with crop spray and crash. The film ends when the reporter and the commander turn up at the memorial service for the three dead astronauts."

"What was the purpose of them proceeding with the mission without the astronauts, and why didn't they just postpone it until they'd fixed the problems with the life support system?"

"The future of the whole Mars program would have been put in jeopardy, or even cancelled altogether, if the mission didn't go ahead on schedule. It will take a death bed confession by Aldrin to ever convince me that man never landed on the Moon!"

"I would have loved to have had the opportunity at one of the conventions he attends to have looked him in the eye and asked him."

"*Hombre a hombre?*"

"Yes, Bert."

"He punched a conspiracy theorist in the face for calling him a coward, a liar and a thief, but he was never prosecuted as it was deemed Aldrin had been provoked."

"I know the one; Bart Sibrel, he used to lie in wait for the men who had walked on the Moon and jump out on them with a bible and ask them to swear on it that they had actually walked on the Moon."

"Yeah, one crazy guy," I replied. "Would you like to borrow the DVD?"

"Well, I would've done but you've told me the plot now, Bert."

"I try my best, pull out all the stops, go the extra mile…"

"Bert!" I turned my head round to face Hugo and recoiled in shock at the horrific sight that met my eyes. Hugo had turned on the AA torch and held it under his chin and the harsh glow of the light casting shadows on his face made it look hideous.

"You nearly frightened the life out of me, you berk!"

"Sorry, Bert, thought it would be a laugh," Hugo said rubbing the back of his hands.

"Are your hands cold?"

"Yes, they're colder than a traffic warden's heart, Bert."

"You know what they say about people with cold hands don't you?"

"Warm heart?"

"No gloves!"

"If I'd have said no gloves, you'd have said warm heart, wouldn't you?"

"Yeah," I said grinning.

"I'm hungry again now, Bert," said Hugo dragging his rucksack towards him and took out the foil covered sandwiches. "Me too," I replied, and rummaged in my rucksack for them. I tore open the foil and removed a sandwich and took a big mouthful, the thick mustard sauce of the piccalilli giving it 'bite'.

"Do you really like banana and brown sauce sandwiches?"

"Yes, they're lovely, Bert, I used to eat them all the time when I was a child. I don't eat them that often but every now and again I get a craving for one, you should try one."

"I think I'll give that treat a miss, thank you, Hugo," I replied as the two of us polished off all four sandwiches in one sitting. I rolled up the foil and threw it on the fire.

Chapter Fifteen

"Is it me, or are the ad breaks getting longer and longer these days?"

"I've noticed that too, Bert. I once counted the number of adverts in a break, and there was the sponsor's advert, twelve adverts for products, an advert for an upcoming TV show and then the sponsor's advert again, plus every time you channel hop to check what's on, most of the time you catch the advert breaks."

"Wow, that's a lot of ads, but a sad hobby, Hugo."

"I wouldn't mind if they were any good Bert, but with a few exceptions they are quite dire."

"Not like the classic ones ay, Hugo."

"No, you can't beat the series of Carling Black Label adverts. The best one was a skit on *The Dambusters* film, where they release a bouncing bomb from a Lancaster bomber and a lone German sentry acts like a goalkeeper and saves it. The Lancaster then drops a further five or so bombs and the German saves them all."

"Yeah, that was a brilliant advert. I remember another one in that series, where a surfer rides the crest of a wave into a pub to that *doo, doo, doo, doo* music from the Old Spice adverts, and when he reaches the bar, he asks for a pint of aftershave!"

"That piece of music, Bert, is called *O Fortuna* by Carl Orff."

"Nobody likes a smart arse," I said with a smile.

"Then, there were the Cadbury's Flake adverts. I think the best one was where a woman was eating a Flake in the bath," Hugo went on.

"Yeah, that Flake woman could make eating a chip butty look sensual." I replied. The Milk Tray man adverts were also good. A rugged James Bond type character wearing a black roll neck jersey and carrying an attaché case containing the chocolates, either leaps off a cliff, runs along the top of a train

or goes over a waterfall in a speedboat amongst other stunts in the series of ads, all to deliver a box of Milk Tray and his calling card of a silhouette of himself and then... leaves!"
"Where's the fun in that, Bert?"
"There isn't any," I replied, shaking my head.
"I used to call one of my girlfriends, Martini, Bert."
"Anytime, anyplace, anywhere?"
"You've heard it?"
"That joke's as old as the ad, Hugo."
"The ones that stick in my mind are the Cadbury's Smash Martians, the Shake n' Vac woman, the Cinzano ones with Joan Collins and Leonard Rossiter and not forgetting the David Soul National Express ads. Most of the modern funny ones seem to be centred on the price comparison adverts, with *Pulp Fiction's* 'fixer' Winston Wolfe, He-Man and Skeletor boogying to a song from the film *Dirty Dancing* and that Italian opera singer popping up everywhere, to save customers from going bananas!"

"The one I'll never forget, though I can't remember the brand of beer they were advertising, was the one with Tubbs Tubbson in it, who got starring roles in films by playing huge parts like a planet or an iceberg, but they soon dried up after he started drinking this particular brand of low calorie beer because he lost weight."

"I never saw that one, Bert, but the one I'll never forget was one that was advertising how local a supermarket chain was, by having a woman say something like "I wish I had some bread", then out of the bottom drawer of one of the units in her kitchen a man holds out a loaf of bread. The woman didn't even bat an eyelid! If that were me, I would be running for the hills!"

"They're not real Hugo, you have to suspend belief with most of them, and don't forget the man from Delmonte."

"He say yes! What about the public information films, Joe and Petunia in my opinion were the best, Joe with a knotted hanky on his head and Petunia with her Dame Edna Everage type specs and a tongue like a roll of wallpaper licking an ice cream."

"In the opening title sequence of one of the series of *Taggart,* there is a shot of DCI Matt Burke licking an ice cream in exactly the same way and it always reminds me of Petunia, it was a shame that they killed them off."

"What!" Exclaimed Hugo.

"Yeah, they killed them off in a 'Worn Tyres Kill' ad."

"I'll have to check that out, Bert, I don't remember seeing that one!"

"Have a look on YouTube when we get back."

"I will! Anyway, I'm bringing out another CD at Christmas, Bert, it's called 'Max's Christmas Cracker' and I think you're going to like."

"Has it got 'Its Christmas Time Again' on it?"

"Yes it has, as I know you like that one."

"Yeah, it's really good. What you should do is put it on YouTube; you could wear one of those Christmassy knitted jumpers."

"Like what Gyles Brandreth wears?"

"Yeah, that's the type and sit in an armchair with a coffee table in front with some mince pies and a glass of sherry, with in the background a fully decorated Christmas tree."

"That's a really good idea, Bert, I'll give that some thought, and yes it's on the CD."

"Oh, good. What about 'Walking Round in Women's Underwear'?"

"That's not a Christmas song, Bert."

"Yeah it is, it's based on the lyrics of 'Winter Wonderland', Hugo."

"I know, I've heard that version, but the answer is still no. But it is full of all your festive favourites and I've penned a song especially for the CD entitled 'I'm Sittin' in me Pants for Christmas', which I will now sing for the first time before a live audience."

"Just me then," I said, looking around just in case someone else had joined us.

"Now it's time for Christmas,
The presents and the snow,
But there's one thing that I like doing,
I think you ought to know,
Some people say I'm crazy,

Some people say I take a chance,
But there's nothing more I like doing,
Than sittin' in me pants,

I'm sittin' in me pants for Christmas,
I'm sittin' in me pants all day,
Some people might say I'm insane,
Some people might say I'm gay,
Whilst everyone else is deckin' out the hall,
I'm sittin' in me pants for Christmas,
And havin' a ball.

I remember one cold winter,
I was sittin' in me pants
Someone looked in the winda,
And gave me such a glance,
Then just as I stood up,
Me pants they fell down,
And by the time I had got to the winda,
A crowd had gathered round,

I'm sittin' in me pants for Christmas,
I'm sittin' in me pants all day,
Some people might say I'm insane,
Some people might say I'm gay,
Whilst everyone else is deckin' out the hall,
I'm sittin' in me pants for Christmas,
And havin' a ball,

When Father Christmas came down the chimney,
He got quite a surprise,
He saw me sittin' in me pants,
With a plate of hot mince pies,
When he saw I'd got the kettle on,
His face lit up with glee,
He then he dropped his sack of toys,
And joined me for a mince pie and a cup of tea,

I'm sittin' in me pants for Christmas,
I'm sittin' in me pants all day,
Some people might say I'm insane,
Some people might say I'm gay,
Whilst everyone else is deckin' out the hall,
I'm sittin' in me pants for Christmas,
And havin' a ball.

Now you've heard my story,
Why not take a chance?
Take a leaf out of my book,
And sit there in your pants,
You might find it strange at first,
That I think is true,
But you'll enjoy sittin' in your pants,
Even when the day is through,

I'm sittin' in me pants for Christmas,
I'm sittin' in me pants all day,
Some people might say I'm insane,
Some people might say I'm gay,
Whilst everyone else is deckin' out the hall,
I'm sittin' in me pants for Christmas,
And havin' a baaaall."

"What do you think, Bert?"
"Yeah, I'm sure lots of people will buy your CD, Hugo," I replied, when I'd picked my jaw up off the ground.
"I will have to send a copy of my CD to someone in the music business."
"What like, Mickie Most?"
"I think he died years ago, Bert."
"Okay, Pete Waterman then."
"No, he's into his trains now."
"Well, there's only one person left, Hugo."
"Who's that then, Bert?"
"I'll give you a clue, *derrr derrr derrr, der da der, der da der.*"
"What, Darth Vader?"

"No, the other Dark Lord…Simon Cowell."

"Funny, aren't you?"

"I like to think so," I replied with a laugh.

"Do you really think we'll see the beast tonight, Bert?"

"Well, you've either frightened it away for good with your singing or attracted it to our location to see what the racket was!"

I checked my mobile phone, it was 00:02, *only six hours left at the most* I thought. I looked up at the full Moon, which was high in the cold, deep black sky, the unblinking age-old stars were very few and far between each other as were the colourless clouds. An aircraft only visible by its flashing red anti-collision lights sailed silently by.

Ordinarily the full Moon didn't bother me but sat here just after midnight in the woods that wore the darkness like a cloak, it had a hypnotic, mystical like glow to it that gave me the creeps and it felt as if the trees were closing in around me. I wasn't very comfortable with the dark, I never had been even as a child and now likewise as a man.

My imagination was working overtime with every noise being amplified making me jump, and the light from the fire creating shadows in the nearby trees that gave shape to your darkest fears and nightmares which made them real and felt that they were advancing upon you. A quick look away would see them retreat back to whatever hell they had come from but if you stared again too long in the same place they would return. I was working hard not to show my fear to Hugo, and I remembered a line from the *Predator* movie 'if you lose it here, you're in a world of hurt'. I shook the fears from my head and thought of Julia and looked forward to the dawn.

The stillness of the night was suddenly shattered by all manner of sounds emanating from the woods; the sharp cracking of branches, twigs snapping and leaves rustling. There was something definitely moving around in the woods heading in our direction. "Maybe it's a fox…or a badger, Bert."

"Bloody big fox or badger by the sound it's making, I replied, just as everything went deathly quiet again. Hugo and I got up out of our chairs and walked the short distance to the treeline, Hugo shone the powerful beam of the AA torch into the trees, but the probing shaft of light revealed nothing and after a minute or two, we returned to our seats.

"Have you ever played in a Royal Naval Association club?"

"No, Bert, just a British Legion club, why?"

"I went to one once, somewhere in the Black Country, my ex-wife Denise and I went to see a friend of hers called Mal Carr sing. Have you ever heard of him?"

"I don't think so, Bert."

"Well anyway, I only remember two things from that night; the first was that there were men, who were probably committee members with large trays full of tots of rum that walked around all the tables handing them out, and the second was that every sentence people spoke ended in the word 'shipmate;' hello shipmate, how ya doin' shipmate, haven't seen ya in a long time shipmate."

"Sounds like the sort of club I should be playing at, Bert."

"Yeah, it was a crackin' night.

Chapter Sixteen

I must have nodded off, as I woke up with a start. I got up out of my chair, had a stretch and then reached down into my rucksack and fished out the bottle of water, took a swig, and then poured some onto my hand and then splashed it over my face to refresh me. As I returned the bottle to the rucksack I heard a twig snap behind me and I immediately straightened up and cautiously turned around, and that's when I saw it standing there, inside the saffron coloured cone of light created by the fire. I rubbed my eyes thinking I must still be asleep and was dreaming, but when I lowered my hands it was still there. I ever so slowly, so as not to spook the creature began to tap Hugo's left foot with my right foot as he too had fallen asleep, but there was no response.

For what seemed like an eternity I stood there rooted to the spot both fascinated and frightened, looking the creature square in the eyes. The noises from the woods faded out, leaving an eerie silence like someone had slowly turned down the volume on a radio, leaving only the sound of my own heavy breathing and the stuttery clicking noise coming from the creature's mouth. The adrenaline inside me was churning like a cement mixer in the pit of my stomach, triggering the lizard part of my brain to kick in; fight or flight, which at this very moment every fibre of my being was screaming at me to get the hell out of here, but I remained there rooted to the spot, unable to move and feeling as if I was wearing a pair of divers boots.

From what I could see by the warm, irregular glow of the fire, it didn't appear to be the growling, snarling monster, with saliva and crimson coloured blood dripping from razor-sharp fangs which could shred flesh and bone effortlessly, and that, any minute now it was going to leap on me like a velociraptor and tear me apart in the blink of an eye, that the newspapers and 'eyewitness reports' had conjured up.

It was really terrifying facing this fearsome hulking creature alone, as it just stood there looking at me making its clicking noise. I could see that it was humanoid and although it was in a stooping posture, I guessed it would be a good foot taller than me if it stood upright, and looked to be completely hairless and had mottled, leathery looking grey skin with a large head that had a longitudinal ridge across the top covered in wart-like nodules with a short forehead above two hooded, close set glaring chili red eyes, a large fleshy nose with flared nostrils and a generous but thin lipped mouth, full of carnivorous looking teeth which had a pronounced overbite on the top set and a strong jawline. Its torso looked slick with sweat although the early morning air was a tad chilly and it had the physique of a bodybuilder with broad powerful shoulders, a puffed-out chest and a slender waist. Its muscled arms were I felt, slightly longer than a human arm and had human like hands but with longer fingers and long nails with sturdy muscular legs and large feet.

My mouth felt dryer than one of Gandhi's flip-flops, and my heart was pounding away ten to the dozen, and felt like any minute now it would rip its way through my ribcage like the chestburster ripped its way out of Gilbert Kane's chest in the movie *Alien*, plus my anus was opening and closing faster than the blink of an eye, making me fearful I was going to void my bowels and, or my bladder, as I didn't have any spare clothes to change into, and here in Black Woods, I learnt the true meaning of being shit scared!

"Hugo," I managed to utter out of the corner of my mouth, just above a whisper, but he had pulled the earflaps of his cap down over his ears and tied them under his chin. I didn't want to shout or shake him as any sudden noise or movement might scare the creature away, but he was totally oblivious to my plight and slumbered on, his club had rolled off his knees onto the ground.

I took a gulp of air to control my breathing and dug my hands into my jacket pockets and found the KitKat Hugo had asked me to save for him. I took it out and with trembling hands removed the red wrapper and broke the block of four fingers into two twos and put the one half into my mouth, making a *yum yum* sound and rubbing my stomach in a circular motion as if trying to coax a small child to eat a spoonful of gloop from a jar of baby food. I stretched out my trembling right hand and offered the other half to the creature, while I noisily consumed my half of the chocolate. The creature cocked its head to one side as if studying my intentions and began to move ever so slowly around the fire towards me and held out its right hand with its long fingers unfurled as if to take the chocolate from me.

"Hugo," I said again, a bit louder,

"Not now, Mimi," Hugo whispered still asleep. I wanted him to witness the creature besides me. If it ran off, Hugo would blame *me* for not waking him up, or say that I had made the whole thing up. I didn't want to use the camera at this stage as the creature might think it was a weapon of some sort or be frightened off by the flash. I furtively moved my right foot ever so gradually over to Hugo's outstretched left foot and gave it a tap again but got no response. Sighing, I tapped his foot twice in rapid succession and he woke up with a start! He rubbed his eyes and then saw the creature in front of us. "Eh…what the feee…," was all Hugo managed to yell before the rest of the sentence died in his throat, as in his haste to get out of his chair, he over-balanced and fell backwards with his feet flailing in the air like he was doing an impression of a dying fly, before crashing to the ground with a heavy thump and then rolled over onto his right side.

With all the commotion, the creature took off, its powerful legs propelling it swiftly into the safety of the trees. I dropped the half bar of the KitKat I was offering to the creature and automatically raised the camera quickly to my eye and took a series of shots in rapid succession at the fast-moving figure while Hugo was scrabbling to get to his feet. Having gotten to his feet, Hugo grabbed the AA torch and ran towards the trees.

"Don't go into the trees!" I shouted. "You'll never find it!" Hugo pulled up short at the tree line and shone the powerful beam through the trees, sweeping it from side-to-side.

"Nothing, Bert," Hugo said as he returned to the campfire.

"Did you get a look at the creature before you toppled over, Hugo?"

"Only for a second," Hugo said panting. "Please tell me you got some photos of it, Bert?" I turned on my camera and pressed the playback button and after noting the camera had timed the photos at 03:17, passed it to Hugo who scrolled through the five photos I had managed to take before it had disappeared into the trees.

"Hmm," said Hugo, passing back the camera. "The first photo is okay, but the rest are a bit blurry, don't you think?"

"What did you expect, Hugo? that creature or whatever it was, was moving at speed after you frightened it off with your dying fly impression!"

"If I frightened it, it sure as hell frightened the living daylights out of me, Bert! Are you sure it was the actual beast and not somebody running around the woods in a monster costume, to fuel this Beast of Black Woods legend?"

"What, like old man Smithers?"

"Old man Smithers!" Hugo exclaimed with a laugh.

"Yeah, if that *were* a man dressed up in a monster costume, he would have to be in the same league as the late, great Stan Winston. No, Hugo, what we witnessed was the real deal!"

"Did the creature make any attempt to communicate with you?"

"Well it was making some sort of clicking noise, but for all the sense it made it might as well have been in Klingon!"

"You can actually learn to speak Klingon online, and there's even *The Klingon Dictionary* you can buy online as well, Bert."

"Hmm, at least we can confirm from the photos that it doesn't have a tail…or wings!"

"Yes, all these little details matter, you better make some notes on the creature's physical appearance, Bert, while they're still fresh in your mind."

"Yeah, I will," I replied pulling out my notebook and pen from a side pocket of my rucksack. I scribbled down what I remembered and passed the notebook to Hugo.

"Did you happen to notice if it was male or female, Bert?" Hugo asked, looking up from my notebook.

"Funnily enough, Hugo, no, I didn't," I replied turning to face Hugo. "I was too busy trying to rouse you rather than looking at its genitalia!"

"That's a very good description, Bert," Hugo said returning my notebook and I added at the end…sex unknown."

"There was an episode of *The Saint* called 'The Convenient Monster' which was set on the shores of Loch Ness. A dog and later a poacher are found with every bone in their bodies broken and with monster sized footprints all around. It transpired that a woman was trying to kill her husband and then sought to blame his death on the Loch Ness monster like the other victims. Simon Templar finds her horrific club and converted boots for making the monster footprints, but she escapes in a dingy into the mist shrouded Loch Ness. A few days later her mutilated body is washed ashore…"

"Yes, makes you wonder, Bert."

"Yeah, I always wanted to stand on the shores of Loch Ness to try and spot the monster, but when I went to the Loch Ness Centre and Exhibition which is near Inverness some years ago now, and after walking around all the exhibits they conclude that the loch could not sustain anything that size, but in the gift shop they sell all kinds of 'Nessie' themed toys and other memorabilia."

"That's tourism for you, Bert."

"It sure is, Hugo."

"Hmm, is there any coffee left?"

"Yeah, there is, is the chair okay?" Hugo righted the chair and sat down on it.

"It's fine, Bert." I picked the flask up off the ground and unscrewed the lid and poured the coffee into the two mugs Hugo was holding out. "There's just enough for one more coffee each," I said as I returned the flask to the ground and took one of the mugs from Hugo and slumped down into the chair, totally spent. My heart was still pounding away from the encounter, but not as much as before, and my legs felt like jelly, but otherwise I was okay. Cradling the mug in both hands, I sipped the hot and very welcome coffee.

"Do you think you can stay awake this time, Hugo?"

"You think it might return?"

"I shouldn't think so now, but it could be watching us."

"What's this Bert?" Hugo asked as he leant forward in the chair, picking something up off the grass. He straightened up, holding up the empty KitKat wrapper in one hand and the half bar of the KitKat in the other, like clues from a murder mystery.

"I was trying to open up some sort of non-verbal communication with the creature by eating one half of the chocolate and offering the other half to it, but I must have dropped it in my rush to get some photos before it fled back into the woods."

"With chocolate, Bert... correction with *my* chocolate!"

"Alright Willy Wonka keep your hair on, I'll buy you another one!"

"I was looking forward to that KitKat with my coffee, Bert," Hugo said, wiping off the bits of grass that had stuck to it and then proceeded to eat it. "I think I will name it Beastly Bert," Hugo added, still munching on his chocolate while pulling a blade of grass from his mouth.

"Oh, by the way, who's Mimi?"

"Mimi?" Hugo replied looking puzzled.

"Yeah, you were dreaming of her before I woke you."

"Oh, that Mimi," Hugo said with a broad smile. "Mimi Rogers, Bert."

"Mimi Rogers, as in Tom Cruise's ex-wife, Mimi Rogers?"

"Yes, that's the one, I'm sure you've got a celebrity crush, Bert."

"Err, let me think..." I pondered. "I quite like Sigourney Weaver."

"Ooh very nice, Bert," Hugo replied in one of his comic voices. Now, whose your quirky celebrity crush?"

"Prob...ab...ly, I would say...the woman from *Criminal Minds* who..."

"I know exactly the one you mean, it's Garcia the technical analyst, am I right?" Hugo answered for me, jumping in before I could finish talking.

"Yeah it is actually, she reminds me so much of Fa..."

"I know, Bert," Hugo said cutting me off mid-sentence again, putting a comforting hand on my shoulder and giving a knowing nod. "I know."

"Okay, so whose your quirky celebrity crush then, Susan Boyle?" I said wiping away the moisture from my eyes.

"No, it's...Miranda Hart!"

"She's not quirky, Hugo, she's just bonkers!"

"I know," replied Hugo laughing.

Chapter Seventeen

I looked at my mobile phone, it was 04:19, the patchy sky was dark and uncaring, and I was beginning to think that the darkness would never end. I just longed for it to be light enough so we could navigate our way out of the woods safely, have something to eat and then get some sleep. "Do you think we're all alone?"

"In the universe, Bert?"

"No, in the woods Hugo," I said shaking my head. "Of course, in the universe!"

"The universe extends billions of light years beyond our solar system, so there's a good chance there's intelligent life living on a planet similar to the Earth, but it's going to be trillions of miles away," replied Hugo looking up at the few visible, nameless stars.

"I just think there has got to be some other intelligent life forms out there, than just us."

"I read somewhere that aliens are humans from the far future, Bert."

"Are you trying to tell me that humans will evolve into aliens, and have hairless grey skin, a small body and a large, inverted egg shaped head, with large black opaque eyes?"

"Something like that, Bert."

"I'll believe it when I see it," I said laughing.

"Do you think that creature was an alien from another planet, or one of them Soviet ape-men 'super soldiers' that's escaped or gone rogue, Bert?"

"You've been watching *World War Weird* again, haven't you?"

"Yes, it's a really interesting series."

"It is, but I haven't a scooby, Hugo. It seemed almost human, in an ape like body like some sort of chimera, hybrid or missing link, whether due to nature or experimentation...as I say I have no idea."

"Yeah, like a Mape; half human, half ape."

"Hmm, like Mant, the half human, half ant from the film *Matinee*."

"I've never seen *Matinee*, Bert."

"Oh, it's set in 1962, during the Cuban Missile Crisis and at the local cinema they are showing *Mant* which is a parody of several low budget sci-fi films of the 1950's. I guess that's another film you'll want to borrow off me."

"Yes, as long as you don't tell me the plot!"

"I'll bring it together with *Capricorn One* when we meet up on Friday."

"Cheers, Bert."

"One thing I do know is, we must absolutely not tell another living soul about the existence of that creature."

"Not even Ruth?"

"No one, Hugo, and that includes Blodwyn!"

"But, those photos on your camera, are our golden ticket, we've hit the jackpot, Bert!"

"Can you imagine what's gonna happen Hugo, if we go public with them?"

"Fame…fortune?" Hugo replied. "If it turned out to be a real alien, we'd be talking telephone numbers!"

"Maybe, but every muckety muck and swinging dick from here to…err…Timbuktu, is gonna descend on these woods. It'll be like that scene from *The Lost World: Jurassic Park* where a band of mercenaries and big game hunters come crashing onto the island in vehicles and quad bikes to round up the dinosaurs for a theme park in California. It will be same here with mobile command centres and helicopters that have searchlights and thermal imaging cameras, professional and amateur hunters, scientists, conspiracy and alien fanatics and probably 'men in black' from some obscure government agency all in pursuit of their own separate agendas who will search the woods with a fine-tooth comb until they find the creature either…dead or alive! And then what are they gonna do with it? Do you remember the end of *Raiders of the Lost Ark*?"

"Yes, they put the Ark of the Covenant in a crate, nail it down, padlock it, label it as Top Secret and then it's stored in a vast warehouse which is crammed full of similar looking wooden crates."

"Exactly, we did what we set out to do, Hugo, we proved the existence of the Beast of Black Woods."

"But only to ourselves Bert."

"Isn't that enough?"

"Where's the fun in keeping something like this to ourselves, we should be telling the world!"

"Okay, okay, Hugo, I don't want us to fall out over this, so I shall make you a deal. If a story gets broadcast or printed that contains concrete proof of what we saw, then we shall go public with our story and photos, but until then we remain *schtum*. Is it a deal?"

"Deal, Bert," Hugo reluctantly agreed, spitting on his hand and holding it out. We both shook hands and clapped each other on the back.

"Don't forget our deal, Hugo."

"Yes, I know, Bert, break the deal, face the wheel." Hugo muttered resignedly. I had lifted the phrase from the *Mad Max Beyond Thunderdome* film. The 'wheel' in our case though, was a small cardboard circle with a cardboard arrow-shaped spinner attached to the centre of the circle with a metal paper fastener. The circle was divided into six segments by a marker pen, with four segments having a written forfeit in it, with two segments having no forfeit which read clockwise; buy the coffees and cakes at our weekly get together for a month, buy the next carvery, no forfeit, buy the beer all night, buy the nachos at our next trip to the cinema and no forfeit.

"What's ET short for, Bert?"

"Extra Terrestrial."

"Because he has got small legs."

"I don't get it, Hugo."

"He is short because he has small legs."

"Very funny," I said, letting out a weak laugh.

"Anyway where exactly is Timbuktu? I've heard of it but haven't got a clue where it is."

"Yes, it's…err…hmm…let me put my thinking cap on." I thought long and hard. "Best I can do is West Africa somewhere."

"Hmm," said Hugo sceptically. "You don't know do you?"

"Yeah West Africa, when Blodwyn comes to pick us up I'll ask her to google it."

"Okay, it sounds a bit like that other place... Kathmandu."

"Now I know that's in Nepal, there's a famous poem about it."

"Yes, 'The Green Eye of the Yellow God', Bert. Would you like me to recite it for you?"

"No!"

"What about 'The Charge of the Light Brigade' by Alfred, Lord Tennyson who also wrote a poem called Timbuctoo?"

"Nooo!"

"I'm starting to feel hungry again now."

"Yeah me too, let's have that porridge."

"Sounds like a plan," Hugo replied. I fished in my rucksack for the mess tins and removed the sachets of porridge while Hugo removed the milk from his rucksack and put it on the ground. I knelt down and ripped the top from each of the six sachets in turn and poured the contents of three into each of the mess tins. Hugo then opened the milk and poured it into the mess tins to just over the level of the porridge and I placed them on the fire as Hugo stowed away the milk. I dug out the two spoons from the side pocket of my rucksack and passed one to Hugo and we both knelt down beside the fire, occasionally stirring the now sweet-smelling porridge. "I love the smell of porridge in the morning, Bert,"

With the porridge starting to bubble we removed the mess tins from the fire by wearing Hugo's gloves on our opposite hands and tucked into it with relish. "If this porridge can get Buzz Aldrin to the Moon and back, Hugo, it can get us through the rest of the night!"

"I must say, Leonard and I always have good food, last week we had coq au vin, Ada. Fancy, we tried that once but there's no room in our mini." I almost choked on my porridge laughing at another one of Hugo's Cissy and Ada sketches.

"Do you have any bush craft skills, Bert?"

"I think we're gonna make it out of the woods alive, Hugo."

"Yes, I know that, I meant if we suddenly found ourselves in a jungle, having crash landed say with just a Swiss, army knife, would you know what to do to survive?"

"Apart from being able to light a fire and how to soothe nettles stings…no!"

"Didn't you learn any survival skills when you were in the RAF?"

"Not a sausage, out of the twenty-two years I was in, I spent the grand total of one night under the stars when I was doing my basic training at Swinderby, and we were all each given a 24-hour ration pack."

"What did that consist of?"

"Well, basically it was a small cardboard box packed with food and other sundries to keep you going for 24 hours. It had things like tea, coffee, sugar and powdered milk; chewing gum, sweets and chocolate; a few sheets of toilet paper, salt, matches and a mini tin opener; a breakfast of oatmeal biscuits, tinned bacon burgers and condensed milk that was in like a small toothpaste type tube; a main meal in three small tins, one had something like minced beef in gravy, one was mixed vegetables and the other was a pudding, but I can't remember what that was now and there were lots of packets of Biscuits, Fruit, to give them their official name, but everyone used to call them 'dead fly' biscuits."

"Why was that, Bert?"

"Cos they looked like they had dead flies in them, rather like Garibaldi biscuits. What about you, do you have any special skills you learnt in the Cubs?"

"It was nearly fifty years ago, but about the only thing I learnt was that when rubbing two sticks together to start a fire, make sure one's a match."

"So, if we happen to find ourselves alone in the jungle, were basically gonna die then, Hugo."

"Yes, but according to you, not from the cold or nettle stings. How did you come to join the RAF in the first place, Bert?"

"Well, there lies a tale, Hugo. I had no plans to join the RAF until my Father who had been fitting out a fruit and veg shop, gave me two tickets to the Fruiterers and Vegetable Society's

Annual Dinner Dance that the owner had given him. My best friend, Barry Lemon was home on leave from the RAF and I asked him did he want to go, and he readily agreed. During the night we got to dance and talk to two girls, the one who had paired up with Barry, asked him what he did, and he replied that he was in the Royal Air Force. The girl who I was with asked me the same question, and I told her I worked in a shoe shop. She did not look at me in quite the same way as the girl with Barry looked at him. It was at that moment I decided to join the RAF, and the very next day, being a Monday as I worked Tuesday to Saturday, I visited the RAF Careers Information Office in London Road, Liverpool and applied to join, and six months later I was on a train to Swinderby to do my basic training."

"Wow, it's strange how life turns out."

"Yeah, it certainly is! My friend, Barry would go on to marry the girl he met that evening, and I was his best man. That one evening altered the whole course of my life."

"It sure did, Bert!"

We finished off the hot, filling porridge and rinsed out the mess tins with some water and then dried them with what was left of the toilet roll.

"Do you get the feeling we're being watched, Bert?"

"Isn't there a song called 'The Night Has A Thousand Eyes?'"

"Yes, sung by Bobby Vee, but I am sure I saw a face looking back at me from the woods."

"It's probably just your imagination, Hugo. You do know the brain is hard-wired to see patterns in randomness, like seeing faces in almost anything don't you?"

"No!"

"Yeah, it's like people who see Elvis in a piece of toast, the man in the moon or the Mars Face. If I were to draw two dots on a piece of paper, say half an inch apart, and then draw a dash half an inch underneath the dots, you would see a face even though it's just two dots and a dash."

"I always see a face in my hoover, Bert"

"It's a Henry, isn't it…or is it a Hetty?"

"It's a Henry, " Hugo replied smiling.

Hugo went unusually quiet and was leaning forward in his chair, his face was emotionless as he stared into the flames of the fire. I thought he might still be brooding over my decision not to take our story and photos to the papers straight away.

"Penny for them, Hugo."

"Breakfast, Bert," Hugo replied rubbing the stubble on his chin.

"Breakfast?"

"Yes, I hope Blodwyn knows of a good 'greasy spoon' around here when we meet up with her."

"Me too, what would you have?"

"Two bacon, two sausages and two eggs, is a given, right?"

"Yeah, it's the law."

"Then I would add a piece of fried bread, mushrooms, black pudding and some beans."

"Toast?" I added.

"Yes, Bert, two slices well browned, a lot of places you go to serve what looks like warm bread, oh, and a large mug of tea to wash it all down with."

"I'm licking my lips already, Hugo. As soon as it's light enough to make our way through the woods safely, we'll set off to rendezvous with Blodwyn." I dug my mobile phone out of my pocket and looked at the time, only twenty minutes had elapsed since the last time I had looked at it. It was beginning to feel like being back on a nightshift at the warehouse I used to work at, where I'm sure the time ran backwards.

"Can you hear that noise, Bert?"

"What does it sound like?" I replied, listening intently. Hugo tapped rapidly on his knees like he had a set of bongos *bum-ba, bum-ba, bum-ba, bum-ba*, the sound rising in intensity. "That sounds like the music from *Predator* when they are in the jungle."

"That's right, Bert."

"No, I can't hear the *Predator* music, but there is a noise coming from somewhere."

"Hmm," uttered Hugo, as he poked the fire with his club, sending a shower of crimson coloured sparks up into the night air."

Chapter Eighteen

The buzz from the woods intensified, as the birds woke from their slumber and entertained us with a melodic symphony of cheeps, chirps and coos of their 'dawn chorus' to herald the coming dawn.

"Might as well finish off the coffee," I said picking up the flask off the ground as Hugo found the mugs and held them out. I drained the flask into the two mugs and stowed it away in my rucksack and took my mug from Hugo. "Do you fancy a game of words that are the same singular and plural?" Hugo asked as he emptied the last of the sugar into his drink.

"What like sheep?

"Yes."

"You're like the male equivalent of that woman from *Eggheads*, aren't you?"

"Judith?"

"No, the other woman."

"What, Daphne?"

"Yeah, that's the one."

"I'm not anything like Daphne, thank you, Bert."

"Okay then, can you name the seven actors who played the Magnificent Seven?"

"Hmm, that's a difficult one, but I will give it a go and start with the easiest...Yul Brynner."

"Yeah."

"Steve McQueen."

"That's two."

"Robert Vaughn."

"Yeah, that's three."

"Charles Bronson."

"Yeah, that's correct."

"Ooh, let me think, Bert...James Coburn?"

"Yeah, that's the five easy ones, you're gonna struggle now if you don't know them."

"Hmm, was one a German actor, Bert?"
"Well done, yes he was."
"I can see his face, but the only name I can come up with is Hardy Kruger."
"Is that your final answer, Hugo?"
"Can I phone a friend?"
"At this hour of the morning?"
"Okay, I give up, and I don't know the name of the seventh one either."
"Horst Buchholz, and the least known of the seven actors...Brad Dexter."
"No, I would never have got them two."
"Daphne would have got all seven!"
"Will you shut up about, Daphne, Bert!"
"Okay, keep your hair on," I replied laughing.

The long awaited dawn didn't exactly wake up with a crack; it was more of a yawn, a scratch and a stretch as its light slowly spread across the sky, changing its colour gradually from charcoal to grey and then to a watery blue. The long night was finally coming to an end with the hazy first strands of daylight and increasing temperature, that took away my fatigue and fear, that the long hours of darkness had brought on.

Hugo stood up and began searching the woodland floor like he'd lost something. "You lost summat?"

"I was looking for footprints," Hugo replied, without looking up.

"I bet you had a pair of them shoes with the animal tracks on the souls, didn't you?"

"Wayfinders, yes I did, and they had a secret compass in the heel. Did you have a pair as well?"

"No, I just remember the ads on the TV. Some of the US special forces in Vietnam wore boots which left an imprint of a human foot so the Viet Cong or whoever wouldn't know there were US troops in the area, but they were not a great success."

"It's amazing what the boffins can dream up. I was looking for footprints as I thought there might be some so you could take some photos of them for further evidence, regarding shape and size."

"And your knowledge comes from earning your tracker badge in the Cubs?"

"It was a different type of tracking, Bert."

"Was there a badge for 'staying awake all night in the woods looking for a monster' badge?"

"Errrrrrrrrr no," Hugo replied smiling,

"And *is* there any footprints?"

"Not a dickie bird, Bert!"

"I didn't think there would be," I answered.

After an hour of talking about anything and nothing, I judged that it was now light enough to make our way back through the woods and meet up with Blodwyn. "Okay Hugo, let's pack up, put the fire out and make our way back to civilisation!"

"I'll take care of the fire, Bert." And before I could say anything else, Hugo had jumped up, unzipped his trousers and was urinating over what remained of the fire in a lazy figure-of-eight pattern, and as his urine hit the hot embers they hissed and fizzed until the fire was out. Hugo then zipped himself up and with his club raked over the ash to ensure it had been fully extinguished. "Jobs a good un, Bert."

"Thanks Hugo," I said shaking my head as I folded up the chairs and put them back into the carrying bags. We then packed our rucksacks and attached the chairs to them before heaving them onto our backs and finding my camera, I opened up the battery compartment again, pushed down on the SD card which made it pop up and then removing it, placed it back into its plastic case before returning it to my wallet and then slung the camera around my neck just in case I saw something interesting to photograph.

"What do you want me to do with the bin bag, Bert?"

"Make sure its tied and leave it there, the place is a lot tidier than what we found it in. Ready, Hugo?"

"I sure am," Hugo replied slinging his binoculars over his head.

"Then saddle up and let's get the hell outta here and get some breakfast!"

"I can taste it already, Bert!"

I had a final look about the site to make sure we hadn't left anything behind or left any litter and then we both headed into the woods.

"Keep your eyes open for any sign of the creature," I said as we tramped along the trail that would take us back to the kissing gate. After about fifteen minutes we passed the pond on our left. "Did you notice if the creature had webbed hands or feet, Bert?"

"No, they weren't, I had a good look at its hands, and they were definitely not webbed, are you thinking it could be aquatic now?"

"Just a thought, Bert," said Hugo looking intently at the pond.

"Like the Creature from the Very Shallow Pond?" I replied. Hugo smiled broadly as we trudged on.

"Hang on a second, Bert, there's something funny about that tree over there by the fence line."

"How funny?"

"Well it looks as if one of the trees is...walking, Bert," Hugo said lowering his binoculars and pointing to a thicket of trees. I took the binoculars from him and raised them to my eyes, trying to adjust the focus. *Bloody cheap binoculars*, I muttered under my breath. I looked for a long time, beginning to think Hugo was seeing things through being tired. I repeatedly scanned the area Hugo had pointed to, and after a while I caught a glimpse of movement in the trees Hugo had indicated.

"That's not a walking tree Hugo," I declared, the binoculars never leaving my eyes. "It's a man in a hooded camouflage suit trying his best to look like a tree!" The suit was predominantly dark green with irregular blurred splotches of light green, dull yellow and dull red; it was like he was wearing a suit made of Autumn and wore a backpack in the same colours. When the man stood still, he merged back into the trees and became invisible, but as soon as he moved, he became visible again under the magnification of the binoculars.

"I had a camouflage jacket like that once, put it down somewhere and I haven't been able to find it since!"

"Have you looked in the shed?"

"Good one Bert," replied Hugo laughing.

I raised the binoculars to my eyes again; it looked like he was stalking something. He stopped suddenly and then raised what looked like a long slender item covered in strips of hessian to his face and then I realised to my horror it was a camouflaged rifle with a telescopic sight!

"He's got a rifle!"

"Let me have a look Bert." I reluctantly handed over the binoculars to Hugo, who scanned the ground between the man and whatever he may be targeting. "I can't see whatever he has got in his sights Bert"' said Hugo as he passed back the binoculars. "Do you think he's stalking our beastie from earlier on?"

"I hope not, Hugo, but what else could it be?"

"Rabbits?"

"No, he's too well dressed and armed to be rabbiting," I replied as I looked through the binoculars at the man, just in time to see him take up an aiming posture and then smoke belched out the muzzle of his rifle and then the sound of the shot rang out, reverberating around the woods, causing a flock of birds to noisily take flight away from a group of trees. If we hadn't have seen the shooter, we wouldn't have had a clue which direction the shooter's shot had come from, and who had now slung his rifle across his back and had started to jog, presumably after what he had shot.

Hugo and I exchanged worried glances, thinking that it could be the creature we saw earlier this morning, and we ran as fast as we could in hot pursuit of the shooter to see what he had shot. Off the trail, the ground was very spongy and uneven with the added hazard of fallen tree trunks we had to zig-zag around and ducking under low hanging branches, all of which retarded our progress, but we pressed on. I had to put one hand on my camera to steady it from swinging wildly as it dangled from my neck.

When we finally caught up with the shooter, he was bending over a reddish-brown big cat that lay motionless on the ground, with crimson coloured blood oozing out of a bullet hole on its right side. I was happy it wasn't the creature lying there but felt sorry for the big cat. It was athletic and powerful looking, with a large round face and erect ears. The head and body looked to be approximately the same length as its long tail.

"Is it dead?" I said, red faced and wheezing from the exertion of running to catch up with the shooter.

"I hope so," he said, turning around to face us, exhaling from a roll-up he held up to his mouth. The shooter had pushed his hood down, and now wore a peaked cap in a much lighter Spring like, camouflage pattern on his head from which a ponytail fell onto the back of his collar. He looked like he was in his thirties with a weather-beaten face that was long, lean and angular which had sharp features rather like a hatchet and sported a thick black bushy beard with prominent ears and alert, piercing bird-like grey eyes which constantly flitted from left to right, surveying everything. I reckoned he'd probably been in the woods for days tracking whatever he was after and the big cat was just in the wrong place at the wrong time.

"What is it?" Hugo asked, bent double with his hands resting on his knees, panting.

"What were you expecting?" Hatchet Face said, his eyes staring intently at us.

"We have no idea," I replied.

"Well it's not the Hound of the Baskervilles."

"Ooh, a crack shot *and* a comedian," quipped Hugo.

"Alright, it's a puma." Hatchet Face replied smiling.

"So, what's a puma doing wandering around a wood in Wales?" I replied.

"It's probably escaped from a wildlife park or zoo."

"Have any wildlife parks or zoos reported losing a puma?" I asked.

"Not as far as I know, or, it could have been somebody's pet and it's either escaped or they've turned it loose because it's gotten too big or they can't manage or afford it any longer, and not reported it to the police because they haven't got a licence to keep a big cat."

"Some pet, Bert, all I had was a hamster and a cat, but not at the same time."

"What was the hamster's name?"

"Yoda."

"You called your hamster Yoda?"

"Yes, it was a toss-up between Yoda and Lord Vader."

"A silly name, that is," I said mimicking Yoda, as I shook my head in disbelief. I used to look after my next-door neighbour's pet hamster called Georgia, when they went on holiday. It was a cute little thing but being nocturnal it used to make a racket during the night, scratching around its cage and playing on the exercise wheel. I hate any sort of noise when I'm in bed, even a ticking clock sends me nuts. I was more than happy to hand it back when they returned."

Hatchet Face took a leather bound, stainless steel hip flask from an inside pocket. "Anyone fancy a nip of whisky?"

"The sun must be over the yardarm somewhere in the world," said Hugo, as Hatchet Face flicked what was left of his cigarette onto the grass and ground his boot on it and then undone the hinged screw-top lid and took a long swig before passing it to Hugo. Wiping the top with his sleeve, Hugo took a swig and grimaced as the heat travelled down his windpipe before passing it to me. I also wiped the top before taking a swig. "Thanks," I said and gave out a short cough as the fiery liquid hit the back of my throat, before passing it back to Hatchet Face.

"What's it been feeding on?" Hugo asked hoarsely.

"Around here, any small animals like squirrels, mice, and rabbits plus birds and possibly some sheep."

"D'ya think this is what the locals believe to be the Beast of Black Woods?" I asked Hatchet Face.

"You've heard the stories, have you?" Hatchet Face replied.

"A few," I said, not wanting to give away the extent of my knowledge was solely confined to Blodwyn's scrapbook.

"It could be," Hatchet Face said, giving nothing away also.

"What brings you to the woods this early in the morning?"

"Well like I said, we'd heard the stories and my friend, and I decided to spend the night in the woods to see if we could spot it."

"And did you see anything?" Hatchet Face enquired, scrutinising my face.

"We saw a lot of squirrels and birds, oh, and a domestic cat but no, it was a complete and utter waste of our time. Can I take a photo of the puma please?" I asked.

"Yes, as long as you promise me it will not be used in any book, newspaper or posted on social media".

"You have my word on that," I replied, and moved closer to the puma to take the photo.

"Have you taken any other photos while you've been in the woods?" Hatchet face asked looking down at my camera.

"Only of my friend here holding the cat we came across yesterday evening, this puma is the first thing we've seen of any interest all night," I lied.

"May I have a look?" Hatchet face asked, sounding more like a command than a question and held out his hand. I reluctantly pulled the strap over my head, turned the camera on and passed it over. Hatchet face took the camera and pressed the button to scroll through the photos, which he did slowly. "Nice pictures of Waterloo, Normandy and…the cat," he said, finally passing back my camera. "Yeah, I went to Waterloo in 2015 for the 200th Anniversary and Normandy on a battlefield tour there last year, I replied, slinging the camera back around my neck. "Well, we'll be on our way now, thanks for the chat."

"Pleasure," Hatchet Face said narrowing his eyes.

We walked back the way we had come not daring to look back at Hatchet Face and picked up the trail to take us back to the kissing gate. "How come he didn't see the photos of the creature on your camera, Bert?"

"They're on a SD card which I removed before we set off back into the woods."

"Good thinking."

"Yeah, I think there's more to that guy than what he appears to be."

"How so?"

"He was shooting to kill! Why didn't he use a tranquiliser rifle or trap it and then arrange for the puma to be transferred to a local zoo?"

"You mean he was tracking the creature, and the puma got in the way?"

"Very possibly, also the puma might have posed a threat to the creature, as I said before, he was far too well dressed and armed, plus when he talked to you his eyes were everywhere else as well."

"Yes, it's a wonder the two didn't come across each other, or more to the point the puma didn't find where we were sitting!"

"Well you *were* wide awake with your club at the ready, wasn't you?"

"Very funny, Bert."

"I can see now why the eyewitness reports in the paper were wildly different!"

"Yes, me too now, some saw the creature, and some must have seen the...puma," reasoned Hugo.

"*Exactement* as Poirot would say!" I replied.

Chapter Nineteen

I pulled my phone from my jacket pocket and looked at the time, it was 06:45. I found Blodwyn's number from the contacts list and pressed to call, Blodwyn answered on the third ring. "Morning Rick," she answered, sounding cheerful.

"Morning B, we're about fifteen minutes away from where you dropped us off last night."

"Okay, I'm leaving now, see you soon," she replied and hung up. I returned the phone to my pocket. "C'mon Hugo, Blodwyn's on her way."

"Breakfast here I come," said Hugo with a big smile while rubbing his hands together and quickened his pace. "Let's head for the chopper," he added, imitating Arnie.

"You'll have to settle for Blodwyn's Opel."

"That'll do," replied Hugo as we finally reached the kissing gate, just as the molten amber coloured Sun, majestically broke free of the horizon with the promise of a beautiful, new day ahead.

We passed through the gate and started to walk back up the tarmac path where hopefully at the end Blodwyn would be waiting for us "Here puss, puss, puss," whispered Hugo as he searched for the cat, which was nowhere to be seen.

We made it to the end of the path, just as Blodwyn drew up and we stowed away our kit in the boot and got in the car.

"So where do you want to go for breakfast…McDonalds?" asked Blodwyn looking fresh and dressed in a turquoise blending to navy blue Swansea City football shirt, sky blue jeans and trainers.

"You read our minds, B."

"Wasn't hard really," Blodwyn said with a smile.

"Well, Hugo is allergic to McDonalds," I fibbed, not wanting to embarrass Hugo about his fear of the Ronald McDonald clown turning up out of the blue.

"I've never heard of anyone being allergic to McDonalds before," laughed Blodwyn.

"Yes, it brings me out in a rash, B." Hugo chipped in, going along with my story. "Is there a greasy spoon type place nearby?"

"I know just the place, it's not exactly a greasy spoon, but I think you both will like it. It's on an industrial estate and only twenty minutes away."

"What are we waiting for, B," Hugo said excitedly.

"Okay, so, how was your night in Black Woods?"

"Yeah, it wasn't too mbad actually. We made it to the clearing and lit a fire, talked about everything and nothing, ate all the food we took, Hugo entertained me with a Christmas song he has written and his knowledge of the group names of animals and words that are the same both singular and plural and we thought about what to have for breakfast. Then when it got light enough to walk back through the woods to the kissing gate, we witnessed a hunter shoot an escaped puma dead and had a chat with him, oh and we left the site a lot tidier than what we found it!"

"Well, if it helped you both to pass away the night."

"A very long night," I said with a yawn.

"Do you know the group name of giraffes, B?"

"Hmm," replied Blodwyn after a while. "I would say neck, a neck of giraffes."

"Bert?"

"Haven't a Scooby," I replied yawning.

"A tower of giraffes," said Hugo with a satisfied look on his tired face.

"You seem extraordinary quiet, Rick," said Blodwyn rubbing my right upper arm.

"I'm just tired as I was awake all night, unlike 'Rip Van Winkle' here, who spent most of the night asleep."

"Did you see anything else in the woods, other than a dead puma?"

"Like the Beast of Black Woods?"

"Well, yes!"

"Not a sausage, we heard a lot of snapping branches, trees rustling, bird and animal noises but thought it was just the local wildlife."

"Or it could have been the puma," Hugo piped up.

"Yeah, it could well have been, I suppose, plus we came across a stray cat, that Hugo insisted I take a photo of him with it."

"That's one for the album, Blodwyn replied with a laugh.

"Hmm, the path to the kissing gate is a right fly-tipping area," I commented.

"Yes, I know."

"Where does the path lead to beyond the gate?"

"Just another housing estate, Rick."

Blodwyn turned into the industrial estate and parked in front of a low, red painted building with Village Farm Café in blue on a white signboard.

Inside, the café had white walls with waist height 'brick wall' wallpaper running along all four sides, a wooden floor with wooden chairs and tables that were covered with red-and-white checked plastic covers. We walked up to the counter and read the small, medium and large breakfast boards. Hugo and I ordered the large breakfast while Blodwyn ordered the small vegetarian one. "Beans or tomatoes?" asked the formidable looking woman with the gruff voice behind the counter, who had long blonde hair and wore a white T-shirt beneath a blue pinny with thin vertical white stripes. "Beans please," we all said.

"Bread and butter or toast?" The blonde asked. Hugo and I plumped for toast, while B asked for bread and butter. "What are you having to drink, Hugo?"

"Tea thanks, Bert."

"B?"

"Coffee please?" I paid for us all and we sat at a table next to some fruit machines, either end of which were the ladies and gents toilets.

"How far away are we from your house, B?"

"Only five minutes, Rick."

"Oh, I've just remembered, can you solve a query for us on your phone please, B?"

"Yes, what is it?" Blodwyn replied taking out her phone from her jeans pocket.

"Find out where Timbuktu is." Blodwyn tapped away on her phone.

"Ancient city in Mali, Blodwyn said looking at her phone.

"Where's Mali?" Hugo asked.

"Next to Algeria and Senegal amongst others in West Africa," Blodwyn explained consulting her phone, which was one of those all singing, all dancing models.

"I'll give you that one, Bert."

"I'll take it, Hugo," I said beaming.

"Haven't you been to Senegal, Rick?"

"Yeah, I had an overnight stay in Dakar, when the VC-10 aircraft I was travelling to Ascension Island in developed a technical fault after refuelling, and we all had to spend the night in a local hotel. We were given some money and told this would get us a meal and a bottle of wine in the hotel restaurant, but most people went out to eat. I tagged along with some other passengers and we found a café and had omelette and chips and a few beers. It was reputed that the local women were only accepting wrist watches for sex. Anyway, the next day the aircraft was fixed, and we took off for Ascension Island and on the flight I was constantly hearing quite a few of the other passengers asking for the time."

"You weren't one of them, was you, Rick?"

"No, B, I wasn't, I was one of the few telling them the time!"

"Wow!" Exclaimed Hugo as the large oval shaped plate was put down in front of him. On the plate was two bacon rashers, two sausages, two eggs, black pudding, mushrooms, fried potatoes, two pieces of fried bread and beans with two pieces of toast on a side plate.

"Now, that's what I call a breakfast," I said as my plate was placed in front of me, which was the same as Hugo's. After a few minutes Blodwyn's vegetarian breakfast arrived on a much smaller plate and consisted of one egg, mushrooms, fried potatoes, two pieces of fried bread, one hash brown and beans with bread and butter.

We all heartily tucked into our breakfasts. "This is brilliant, B," said Hugo, spearing a sausage with his fork.

"I'm glad you're enjoying it, Hugo."

"That breakfast was deeelicious," I announced sitting back in my chair rubbing my belly, while watching an old man as he staggered into the café. He looked as if he had had one too many, and as he was making his way around our table, he suddenly lurched to his left, straight into the back of Hugo, who was sipping his tea. Hugo's teeth crunched onto the rim of his cup and he spat out a mouthful of the tea. "Sorry guys," the man said immediately in a slurred, croaky voice. "I've had a few drinks and I just want a coffee."

Hugo mouthed a curse as he wiped himself down with a napkin as the old man managed to stagger over to the empty table next to ours and flopped down onto a chair. He looked dishevelled and must have been in his late sixties, early seventies and was unshaven with red-rimmed watery eyes, set in a deeply lined craggy face with a purple bulbous nose and yellow teeth which kept on chewing on something, though I swear his mouth was empty and only stopped when he was talking. A half-smoked cigarette was tucked behind his left ear.

Over a frayed white shirt, he wore a black double-breasted pea jacket with what looked like last night's dinner down the front and a navy-blue Breton fishermen's cap, which gave him a nautical look, together with blue jeans and black slip-on shoes.

"I'm Bill," the old man slurred.

"Hi Bill, we all replied together.

"Sorry to interrupt you guys, sorry, but have you ever heard of Area 51?" Bill unexpectedly said.

"Yes, we have," answered Hugo excitedly. Area 51, is the name given to the top secret USAF facility in the heart of the Nevada desert which was alleged to house live aliens and for developing new weapons and aircraft by reverse engineering alien technology from downed UFOs; but from the many documentaries I'd seen the facility was used for the operational development and testing of classified experimental projects like the Lockheed U-2 high altitude reconnaissance aircraft, though Hugo would disagree.

"Do you know what they are hiding there?" Bill replied, who now had our full attention.

"Err...no," answered, Hugo again.

"Neither do I," stated Bill, matter-of-factly and held open his arms. We all looked at him speechless, with our mouths wide open. There followed a deathly silence and in my mind I heard a lone, sad toll of a church bell together with a hollow howling of wind. "I'm seventy-two, you know, but I can tell you what's not there," Bill added, breaking the silence.

"Okay, so what's not there," I said as Hugo was still picking his jaw up off the floor.

"Aliens," Bill replied casually.

"There are no aliens at Area 51, okay, so what do *you* think is going on there then?" Hugo cut in, having recovered his power of speech.

"I could do with a coffee," Bill said licking his lips and got up and unsteadily walked over to our table and plonked himself down in the empty chair next to Blodwyn. Hugo and I looked at each other as Blodwyn got up from the table. "Would you like anything to eat?"

"No, just coffee thank you...thank you."

Blodwyn got up and walked over to the counter and returned with a cup of coffee and placed it down in front of the old man together with some sachets of sugar and a spoon.

"Thank you, thank you," Bill said tearing off the tops of the sachets and pouring the sugar into his coffee, with breath that could penetrate the frontal armour of a Tiger Tank. He then reached into the right pocket of his jacket and pulled out a brown paper bag and looking furtively around the café to check nobody was looking, quickly unscrewed the top off the small bottle inside and poured a generous amount of the golden liquid into his coffee cup, which I assumed was whisky, replaced the top and returned it to his pocket then stirred the coffee, raised it shakily to his mouth and took a deep gulp of the alcohol laced coffee then sat back in his chair.

All three of us just sat there looking at the man attentively, waiting for him to say something. Bill looked at us in turn wiping his mouth with his sleeve. "But, what I can tell you is that all these probes they're sending out into outer space, aren't looking for alien life forms," Bill said almost in a whisper as he gazed out of the window and looked up at the grey-blue sky.

Hugo followed his gaze out of the window, shook his head, and then returned his attention back to the old man.

"What do *you* think they are looking for?" Hugo asked quietly.

"Minerals," Bill replied again in a whisper, leaning forward conspiratorially towards Hugo.

"Minerals!" Hugo exclaimed raising his voice, taken aback by the old man's answer.

"What sort of minerals?" I whispered back.

"Gold, silver, platinum, titanium, nickel, iron and a whole load of other minerals I've never heard of before and now can't remember," Bill replied taking another gulp of his coffee.

The sound of a cup shattering on the floor, having fallen off a piled up tray of crockery being carried by a member of the café staff, made us all jump.

"Sack the juggler!" A man sat at one of the other tables hollered over the cheering of the other customers.

"Yes well, I think we must be off now," said Blodwyn getting up from the table. "I bet you two will want to have a power nap after last night."

"Yeah, I'm feeling quite tired now," I replied.

"Me too", added Hugo with a yawn.

"Thanks for the most interesting chat," I said to the old man who was draining the last of his coffee.

"Pleasure talking to you all, and don't forget about the minerals," the old man said croakily with a wink while tapping his nose with his shaking right index finger.

"Wales is getting weirder and weirder each day," remarked Hugo as we left the café. "And thanks, Bert, for not letting on about my fear of clowns to Blodwyn," added Hugo out of earshot of Blodwyn

"That okay, no problem."

Chapter Twenty

After a few hours' sleep and a shower, I was right as rain. It didn't pay to have too much sleep as it would be difficult to sleep this evening. Hugo was up already, enjoying a cup of coffee and wearing a shirt that looked as if it was made out of Smarties.

"Afternoon, Bert," Hugo said a little too loudly.

"Afternoon, Hugo," I replied, with a yawn.

"Good sleep?" Enquired Blodwyn.

"Like a log," I answered.

"How do you fancy going to Barrybados, Blodwyn asked a bit more quietly. "It's not very far away in the car."

"Is it a bit like Skegvegas?"

"Yes, Hugo, but much better," replied Blodwyn with a laugh, or there's the Festival Park Owl Sanctuary?"

"Isn't Barry where they filmed *Gavin and Stacey*?" Hugo asked.

"Yes, that's right, you can visit all the locations of the series, it's a great day out, plus it's right on the beach, and we can get some fish and chips."

"Yeah, sounds good to me, I think we'll leave the owls until next time, B," I said with a smile.

"I'll hold you to that, Rick," Blodwyn replied with a wink.

After a coffee we were ready to go. "Do you wanna sit in the front, Hugo?" I asked.

"No, it's okay, Bert, I'm quite happy in the back, thanks."

"Okay," I replied

"Fire up the Opel!" Hugo cried from the back, as we set off for Barry.

"If you look to your right now, you will see a Gothic fairy tale castle," said Blodwyn as we motored along the M4. Hugo and I looked over to the right and on a wooded hillside partially hidden among the trees was indeed what looked like a fairy tale castle. From what I could see of it, it had circular stone towers of different heights topped with conical roofs with what looked like a weathervane on top. "What's it called?" asked Hugo.

"Castell Coch, which means Red Castle," answered Blodwyn. "It was built in the 1870's on the foundations of a 600 year-old castle by the third Marquess of Bute and episodes of *Doctor Who* and *The Sarah Jane Adventures* have been filmed there."

"I will have to look that up when I get back home," replied Hugo.

Forty-seven minutes later Blodwyn parked the car on the gravel parking area, which overlooked the sea and paid the parking charge with her card. As I got out of the car I had a big stretch in the warm sunshine, and the three of us crossed the road and came upon a row of shops.

I desperately needed to use the toilet and have another coffee. The first café we came across we went in. To our left was a woman with short purple coloured hair and an orange hoody, sat on a sofa with a dog on her lap which started to bark at Hugo.

"It's the hat," said the woman to Hugo. "He doesn't like hats." Hugo immediately took off his beige NGK logoed baseball cap and walked over to the Jack Russell and stroked it. "What's his name?" Hugo asked.

"Murphy," replied the woman. While Hugo played with the dog, Blodwyn bought the coffees and I went to the toilet.

It wasn't until I'd sat down at the table with Hugo and Blodwyn that I realised we were in a dog friendly café called 'K9 Plus 1, Paws for a Coffee'; with dog salt and pepper pots, dog sugar sachet holders, dog menu holders and dog wallpaper together with pictures of dogs on the walls and a bone-shaped sign that read 'Beware of dog kisses'. "What would be nice with the coffee would be a free biscuit shaped like a bone," Hugo said.

"That's a good idea," Blodwyn replied. "Why don't you have a word with the owner?"

"I shall send him an email."

A blonde haired woman in a lemon yellow waterproof hooded jacket was pushing a much older but lively woman in a wheelchair which was probably her mother towards the exit, as they drew level with our table the elderly woman who was wiping her nose with a tissue, started to get excited and was waving to us all. We all smiled broadly and waved back.

"You're lucky she didn't offer you some cake," the younger woman said with a smile.

"I love cake," Hugo replied. "In fact, we all do." Both women smiled and waved as they left the café.

Drinks finished, we left the café and went next door into the Hypervalue store, which was like a Wilko's, Poundland and beach shop rolled into one and sold Welsh gifts, items of clothing, everything you needed for the beach; buckets, spades, hats, sunglasses, inflatables, sun cream, beach towels etc., *Gavin and Stacey* merchandise together to my surprise some Scotland and Edinburgh mugs!

We took our time perusing the shelves. I bought a red cup with 'Sugar Tits' on it in white which was a phrase used by Dave the coach driver in *Gavin and Stacey*, two sticks of rock in Fruity Rainbow and Pasty flavours while Hugo bought a T-shirt with 'Oh! What's occurring' another phrase used in the show by Nessa which also had her picture on it, some Dinosaur flavoured rock and a joke egg which looked like the real thing but was made of a hard rubber. Blodwyn didn't buy anything.

Further along we came across the Treasure Island Arcade, which had outside the entrance large figures of a gorilla, panda and a bear. "Take a photo of me, Bert," Hugo said passing me his mobile phone as he walked towards the gorilla, whose right hand formed a seat.

"You're such a child," I replied as Hugo was sitting in the gorilla's palm with a cheesy grin plastered across his jovial face. Photo taken I gave Hugo back his camera who laughed heartily at the image and showed it to Blodwyn who also laughed.

Behind the Smugglers Cove Adventure Golf Course was a RNLI visitors centre and shop. We all went in and had a look around. In the shop I bought a pin badge to add to my growing collection of pin badges from wherever I went, rather like people collecting thimbles. When I return home, I will pin it on my special 'pin badge' beany hat.

The Western Shelter was an open concrete structure with nine bays divided by paired Tuscan columns which rested on the sea wall which spanned the seafront, overlooking the hazy and cold looking waters of the Bristol Channel which washed against the caramel coloured sand of the bustling beach, where amongst the crowd was a metal detectorist combing the beach and a young girl in a pink baseball cap with her long blonde hair tucked through the rear, wearing a black crop top exposing her midriff, black leggings and pink trainers; her dog was enthusiastically running ahead of her, attached by its lead to the right handlebar of her Segway, which was gliding along the granular surface of the beach like a Roman chariot at the Circus Maximus.

Inside the shelter was Zio's gelataria, The Beach Shop, Island Leisure Amusement Arcade and three fish and chip shops. We just managed to find an outside unoccupied table with three chairs at the middle chip shop, the very busy Boofy's Chip Shop which had the tag line 'The Codfather of Sole', whose logo featured a hat wearing, cigar smoking and tommy-gun toting green fish and was said to be the chippy of choice for the cast of *Gavin & Stacey*. What are the fish and chips like, B?" Hugo asked.

"Really nice," replied Blodwyn. We all decided to have fish, chips and mushy peas. I gave Hugo a twenty-pound note and Hugo and Blodwyn disappeared into the shop. After about fifteen minutes they returned with our meals, together with mugs of tea and blue three-pronged plastic forks and white plastic knives. We all tucked into our meals with gusto.

"St. Athan can't be very far from here, B, can it?"

"No, oh…must be about seven miles west along the B4265, Rick, it's a MOD unit now."

"I didn't know that," I replied.

"Is this the place that they hold the Elvis Festivals, B?" Hugo asked.

"No, they're held at Porthcawl, which is about forty minutes from here by car. It's actually the world's biggest Elvis Festival, and the whole town goes Elvis crazy over the weekend. I've been once and it's really good, the next one is in two weeks' time."

"Are you going to go?"

"If I were a hard-core Elvis fan, Hugo I would, but I only went to see what is was like the year before last. When you come again, we will have to go and visit Captain Beany."

"Who on earth is Captain Beany?" Hugo and I replied.

"You've never heard of Captain Beany?" Blodwyn answered surprised.

"Errrrrrrrrr no," we both replied in unison.

"He's a legend, he lives in Port Talbot, and is a bit shall we say…eccentric, but he raises a lot of money for charity and has turned his council flat into a museum dedicated to baked beans."

"We've got to go and see that next time, Bert!"

"Yeah, sounds like fun, a museum about baked beans," I replied with a smile.

Blodwyn pulled out her mobile phone from the back pocket of her jeans and furiously tapped away on the keys. "Yes, the Baked Bean Museum of Excellence," she read from the screen.

"How far is that from your house, B?"

"Nine miles," Blodwyn replied, after tapping the keys of her phone again.

"While you're on your phone, can you find out where pomegranates come from please?"

"Bit random, but yes, Rick."

"I've just remembered we were talking about pomegranates on the coach, and we just wondered where they come from?"

"They originated in an area between Iran and northern India and are also grown throughout the Mediterranean, South Asia and the Middle East, and now are also grown in parts of California and Arizona."

"Ooh, very interesting," I replied while Hugo nodded his head.

"Anyway, getting back to places to visit, there's also the Big Pit and the National Roman Legion Museum."

"What's the Big Pit?" Hugo asked.

"It's the National Coal Museum at Blaenafon, where you can go down in the cage and have an underground tour of a coal mine. I've only been once, you get kitted out with a helmet and a head torch and have to hand in at the beginning anything that has a battery in it like mobile phones or car keys, but it's really good and gives you a taste of the work and conditions of a Welsh coal mine."

"That sounds very interesting, Bert."

"Yeah, and I like the sound of the National Roman Legion Museum."

"I haven't been there, but it has the remains of a Roman Legionary barracks and an amphitheatre. I've got some leaflets at home you can take away with you."

"Great, thanks," I replied.

"I'm stuffed now," said Hugo rubbing his stomach and downing the last of his tea.

"Me too, that fish was massive," I replied.

"Yes, I'm as full as an egg," B said laughing. "Okay, you've got to go in The Island Leisure Amusement Arcade, it's where Nessa used to work in *Gavin & Stacey*." We cleared the table and put the rubbish in the bin and followed Blodwyn in, past the Postman Pat and Spacebike kiddies rides.

It was full of arcade games; slot machines, two pence coin 'pusher' machines, cuddly toy 'grabber' machines and more. Hugo immediately made his way to one of the grabbers and put a coin in the slot. "I love these," Hugo said pushing the up/down buttons to try and grab one of the soft toys and the left/right buttons to swing it over the hole hopefully with a Teddy. After four more attempts he gave up.

"It would be cheaper to buy a cuddly toy than try and get one with the grabber," said Blodwyn.

"I know, but this way is a lot more fun."

At the actual change kiosk in the arcade where Nessa worked there was an orange circular sign on the glass partition which read 'Gavin & Stacy Fans Sorry! Nessa has the day off…'.

After a leisurely walk along the beach with an ice cream, we headed back towards Blodwyn's car. "Thank you for bringing us to Barrybados, B," I said.

"Yes, it has been lush," Hugo added with a laugh.

"My pleasure, how do you fancy spag bol with Parmesan cheese and garlic bread for dinner tonight?"

"Yes please, B," we both replied.

Chapter Twenty-one

As usual, Hugo was sitting having a cup of coffee as I wandered into the dining room after a good night's sleep. "Morning."

"Morning, Bert."

"Morning, Rick, did you sleep well?"

"Like a baby, thanks."

"Good, here's those leaflets on the Big Pit and Roman museum," replied Blodwyn looking refreshed and cool in a white blouse and black jeans.

"Thanks, B."

"This morning, I thought I'd make you a Welsh treat before you go back," said Blodwyn as she placed a plate each in front of Hugo and I and a coffee for me. "*Paws Cob*," she added. I looked down at the plate which looked like cheese on toast, but guessed it was Welsh Rarebit. "Thank you, B," Hugo and I said together and tucked into the snack. "What's in it B?" I asked.

"In a bowl you cream some butter, then stir in salt, Cayenne pepper, Worcestershire sauce, mustard, cheese and either milk or beer. I have used milk, then you toast bread on one side and then spread the mixture on the untoasted side and pop under the grill until brown and *voila*, *Paws Cob*, or as you say, Welsh Rarebit."

"What's that you've got, B?" Hugo asked tucking into his toasted snack.

"It's a beetroot and salad cream sandwich."

"Sounds lovely for breakfast," replied Hugo pulling a face.

"It is actually!"

After our lovely breakfast Hugo and I returned to our rooms to get our bags. I opened mine and pulled out a tin of jack fruit that I bought in Tesco on Sunday and left it on the chest of drawers for Blodwyn to find, it was an 'in' joke between us. I checked around the room and in the bathroom to make sure I hadn't left anything and joined Blodwyn and Hugo downstairs and then we left the house for the short journey to the coach station.

Blodwyn parked the Opel in the little car park at the rear of the National Express Ticket/Information building, forty minutes before our coach was due to depart. Blodwyn got out of the car and opened up the back and we removed our bags.

"Thanks for everything, B, we've both had a great time," I said giving Blodwyn a *cwtch* and a kiss on the cheek. "I'd be really interested if any more Beast of Black Woods stories appear in the papers, could you send me a copy please?"

"Yes, I will scan the page and email it to you, Rick."

"Thanks, B."

"It has been a fantastic few days, thank you, B," said Hugo also giving Blodwyn a *cwtch* and a kiss on each cheek.

"My pleasure, don't leave it so long next time."

"We won't," we both replied in unison as we picked up our bags.

"Oh, and give me a phone, Rick, to let me know you've got back okay."

"I will," I replied, as Hugo and I returned Blodwyn's wave as she drove out the car park.

We used the toilets and then sat down on the benches adjacent to the coach bays, as there was nowhere to sit at the actual coach bays. "I'm just going to see which bay our coach is due in on." I said, sauntering towards the coach bays.

"Okay, Bert."

"Birmingham?" A guy in an orange Hi-Viz vest said as he approached me.

"Yeah."

"The coach has had to divert around an accident, so will be about 20 to 25 minutes late, and will depart from Bay 5 after the Heathrow coach departs."

"Okay, thanks," I replied and sauntered back to Hugo.

"It's due in on Bay 5, after the coach to Heathrow leaves, but has been delayed due to an accident."

"How long?"

"The man reckons 20 to 25 minutes."

From where we were sat, we could see the coaches as they entered the coach park and after twenty minutes the NX332 turned up. We grabbed our bags and headed for Bay 5 and joined the rest of the waiting passengers. The coach said it was for Hull, calling at Birmingham, Nottingham and Doncaster. After having our ticket checked and our bags stowed in the hold, we boarded the coach and found two empty seats at the back opposite the toilet and fastened our seatbelts.

The coach pulled out at 13:05. The guy in the opposite seat was wearing headphones and watching a film on his mobile phone.

"So, what did you think of our trip to Wales?"

"Apart from it being a cross between *The X Files* and *Eerie Indiana*, Bert?"

"Yeah, it was a bit on the weird side at times," I snickered.

"Yes, I loved every minute and B and Bu are such lovely people."

"Good, I'm glad you enjoyed it and yes they are."

The driver pulled into the Newport stop at 13:35, nobody got off and ten people got on, including an elderly woman with a very large dayglo orange bag that she placed gently on a seat nearest the aisle and sat on the adjacent aisle seat in front of us as both window seats were occupied and she explained to the passengers that it contained a cake.

"What sort of cake is it?" Hugo asked leaning forward through the gap in the seats.

"It's a Spiderman cake, I've made it for my grandson's sixth birthday tomorrow."

"That will get his Spidey senses tingling," exclaimed Hugo.

"Indeed," replied the woman with a big smile.

The coach travelled along the M5 and at 14:35 pulled into the Worcester stop where two people got off and nobody got on.

My mobile phone suddenly started to ring, and I dug it out of my pocket "Hello," I answered.

"Is that Mr Shannon?" A female with a soft melodic voice asked.

"Yes it is."

"According to our records, you have been involved in a motor acc..." I cut her off in mid-sentence and returned the phone to my pocket.

"Not the tax office again, Bert, saying they have issued another arrest warrant for tax fraud?"

"No," I laughed, "Not this time, motor accident, I've told them until I'm blue in the face I haven't been involved in an accident and if I had, I would be phoning *them* and to delete my number from their records, but they still phone me, so I just cancel the call now and block the number, plus there's the calls to say my washing machine warranty is about to expire!"

"You haven't got a washing machine, Bert!"

"I know, I use the launderette!"

"M5 The North and Birmingham," Hugo commented as the sign flashed by on our left.

"Jolly dee, I replied.

"You know people have bucket lists, Bert."

"Yes," I replied.

"What exactly *is* a bucket list?"

"It's a list of things you would like to do before you err 'kick the bucket' so to speak, like do a parachute jump or travel to say…India or somewhere."

"I will have to start one."

"What would be on your list?"

"Hmm, I would like to go up to Midge Ure, look him in the eyes and say 'ah shaddup-a your face,' Ure!"

"Well, I hope I can prise him off you in time before you lose consciousness as he shakes you warmly by the throat!"

"Thanks, Bert."

"No problem, but I'd have thought you would've liked to have tracked down Billy Shears or appeared on *Britain's Got Talent* before you tackle Midge?"

"Do you think Midge has ever met Joe Dolce, Bert?"

"I seriously doubt it," I replied with a laugh.

"Yes, I will add them to my list plus I would love to appear on *Bargain Hunt*, sing with a big band and I would love to go to America."

"Anywhere in particular?"

"Hmm…New York for a start I think.

"Very nice," I replied.

"Have you got a bucket list, Bert?"

"Not as in a written list as such, but I can cross off immediately spending a night in the woods!"

"Me too!" replied Hugo smiling.

"I've done a few things I always wanted do, like visiting America and parachuting. While I was waiting by the aircraft door ready to jump, I turned to the guy behind me and said, 'what was the name of that Indian again'?"

"I don't get it, Bert."

"What do people shout when they jump out of an aircraft?"

"Help?"

"No, they shout Geronimo!"

"Oh right, Bert, I met this Native American once, who introduced me to his wife called Four Horses, I said to him that's a beautiful name, what does it mean? He replied nag, nag, nag, nag!"

"Anyway," I said trying not to laugh as Hugo laughed himself silly at the joke. "I've always wanted to be a film and TV extra, visit Glasgow, go up in a hot air balloon, ride a horse and also write a book."

"What sort of book?"

"Probably a non-fiction book about badges."

"Badgers!"

"No, Hugo," I replied, shaking my head. "have I ever since we've known each other, had even the remotest interest at all in badgers?"

"Err no, Bert!"

"Well there you go; I mean military cloth *badges* from the First World War."

"Very interesting, Bert, I have *also* been toying with the idea of writing a book."

"Oh nice, about what?"

"Don't laugh, a walking, talking chest of drawers, and in the drawers are all sorts of items that come in handy on his adventures."

"What like some sort of *Inspector Gadget*, but made out of wood?" I answered, biting my lower lip.

"Something along those lines, yes."

"Yeah, that sounds like a wacky but interesting concept, I must say, Hugo," I replied, taken aback by the sheer incredulity of it, while arching my right eyebrow that Roger Moore would have been proud of. "Have you come up with a name for it yet?" I added.

"No not yet, I'm still working on that."

"What about Chester Drawers?" I proffered.

"I see what you did there, Bert, and yes…it is…brilliant! Can I use it?"

"Yeah, crack on," I replied as I looked out the coach window and caught a quick glimpse of a sign that read Birmingham 27 miles.

I must have dropped off as Hugo was calling Bert repeatedly, and I woke up in time to hear the driver announce over the tannoy to say that he would be taking a break at Birmingham and that all passengers going forward on this coach are to be back on board no later than 4pm, just as the coach pulled into Bay 9 of Digbeth Coach Station at 15:41. We waited in the queue to get off the coach, picked up our bags and headed into the coach station. "I'll get the coffees, Bert."

"Okay, make mine a large one please, I'll go and see what bay the Leicester coach leaves from, I'll meet you by the toilets." I looked at the overhead departures monitor, but it didn't show our coach yet, so I headed to the information desk.

"What bay does the 16:15 departure for Leicester leave from please?" The young brunette tapped the keys of her computer and looked at the screen. "Service 339 from Bay 15/16," she said looking up with a smile.

"Thank you," I replied, returning the smile and headed towards the toilets. Near the toilets was a snack vending machine which had KitKats inside. I put the coins in and retrieved the chocolate bar and put it in my jacket pocket and entered the toilet after paying the 30p fee.

Hugo was waiting with the coffees as I exited the toilets.

"Bay 15/16," I said. We walked along the row of bays and found ours were the last set of bays in the station and we sat down on the only seats available facing the bays next to a tired looking curly haired man. The 339 was sat in Bay 15 but there was no sign of the driver.

"How's it goin' now?" Curly said with an Irish accent.

"Yes, we're fine thanks, and you?" Hugo replied.

"Ah, not so good. I came over from Belfast yesterday to meet a man at *The Bull* statue in the centre of town at 10 o'clock this morning, but he didn't turn up."

"If you don't mind me asking, what were you meeting him for?" I asked.

"He had some pigeons for sale, and we were gonna go back to his place so I could view them."

"Couldn't he have brought them to the meet at *The Bull* to save you some time?"

"Ah no, he'd have brought any four wee pigeons. I wanted to go and view them myself and pick the four that *I* wanted, but as I say I waited around for two hours and he never turned up."

"Didn't you have his phone number, or he yours so you could contact each other if anything went wrong or if you or the man were delayed?"

"Ah no, we were just supposed to meet at the statue at 10 o'clock, now I'm going home with no pigeons." Hugo and I looked at each other nonplussed.

"So how do you get home from here?"

"I get the coach from here to Stranraer and then the ferry to Belfast."

"Stranraer!" Hugo cried.

"How long will the coach take to get to Stranraer?" I asked astounded.

"About ten hours," Curly replied wearily. "But I'll sleep most of the way."

I watched as the driver turned up and did something inside the coach then climbed out and standing by the bay door called forward those passengers that had originally been on the coach and then the passengers joining at Birmingham. We said goodbye to Curly and wished him a good journey and joined the queue. With our ticket checked and bags stowed away, we boarded the coach and sat down in the middle of the coach on the left-hand side and fasted our seat belts.

Chapter Twenty-two

The coach pulled out at 16:17, two minutes behind schedule, after the usual safety brief.
"Here, I got you a present," I said handing Hugo the KitKat.
"Thanks, Bert, replied Hugo, genuinely surprised and unwrapped it immediately and ate it noisily. Good job the woman in the window seat in front of us had earpieces in as she rocked her wet looking long black hair backwards and forwards while the two men in the seats opposite were also noisily eating crisps.
The coach crawled its way through Birmingham city centre and then picked up speed once we hit the M6. "What are you writing, Bert?"
"Just a little something for Julia."
"A love poem?"
"Something like that."
"Give me a look, Bert?" I sighed as I reluctantly passed over the spiral bound notebook bearing my innermost thoughts about Julia to Hugo, who pretended to clear his throat and read it out quietly.

"In my world you are my Sun,
And I don't mind if in your world I am your Pluto,
I am just over the Moon, that we revolve around each other,
As the warmth of your glow,
Lights up my world."

"That's beautiful Bert, it really is, can you write something for me like that," Hugo said, passing me back the notebook.
"I like you, Hugo, but not in that way," I said trying my best not to laugh.
"Not for me you berk, for me to give to Ruth!"
"Oh I see," I said laughing. "I thought you were a songwriter?"

"I am, but of comedy and Christmassy songs, Bert, not love songs."

"Oh right, anyway, how come you call Ruth by her proper name and not, Bertie?"

"Because I always associate Bertie with Melody, plus Ruth told me not to call her, Bertie!"

"Sensible woman, okay, I will give it a go." I thought for a while, before starting to write, and after about five minutes or so, I tore the page out from my notebook and passed it to Hugo, who again read out the words quietly.

"I would capture the night stars for you,
And fashion them into a necklace,
But they would not shine as brightly as your eyes, Ruth,
So, I got you this teddy bear charm instead."

"That's also beautiful Bert,' said Hugo, and though he would never admit it, his eyes had moistened.

"No probs."

"I had to put my foot down with Ruth the other night, Bert!"

"Oh, why was that?"

"She said I looked like a flamingo!"

"Very good," I replied, with a smile creasing my mouth.

"Here's one for you, a man goes to the doctors and says doctor I think I'm a moth. The doctor replies it's not a doctor you want, it's a physiatrist. The man replies, I was on my way to the physiatrist's, when I saw your light on."

"Good one," said Hugo with a guffaw. "Would you like me to recite you a poem, Bert?"

"Is it 'The Charge of the Light Brigade', by Alfred, Lord Tennyson?"

"Err... no, it's 'The Train Spotter', by my good friend, Raven Black."

"Raven Black!" I said astonished. "Is she a Goth per chance?"

"She is actually, but only at weekends."

"Hmm, that would be like Blodwyn saying she's a pescatarian, but only at weekends!"

"Raven is a top banana at some big firm, so has to dress sensibly during the week."

"Where do you know her from then?"

"She's a fellow 'cluester', Bert"

"Oh right, and how is the search for the elusive Billy Scissors progressing?"

"It's Billy Shears as well you know, Bert, and no, we are no nearer to finding him at the moment, but we will, it's only a matter of time. Anyway, I give you 'The Train Spotter' by Raven Black."

"Jolly dee."

"As your standing on the platform,
Excitement fills the air,
You're waiting for the chuff chuff,
And you haven't got a care.

You've reached into your wardrobe,
To dress and look the part,
Some people say you look a pratt,
Some would say quite smart.

A nice blue zipped up anorak,
With a fur edged snorkel hood,
A little canvas shoulder bag,
With flask and pen and book.

Some comfy Jesus sandals,
Showing diamond sided socks,
And the static from your trousers,
Gives your legs electric shocks.

And when you get to New Street,
Feeling slightly hotter,
You're welcomed by your lookalike friends,
Who say hiya fellow train spotter!"

"That's actually very good, Hugo, how do you manage to remember all the words?"

"I'm a singer, Bert, you have to be good at remembering words. I know word-for-word at least thirty songs."

"Wow, that's impressive!"

"Yes, it's not bad. Ruth asked me once could I stop singing 'Wonderwall' all the time."

"And?"

"And, I replied maybe!"

"Very good," I said laughing. "Did I ever tell you about one of my work mates who was in a band?"

"No, Bert, you didn't."

"Yeah, Colin his name was, and he was always bangin' on about how they were booked solid for the next three months. Then one day he brought in a photo of his 'band' and there was Colin playing the drums in a round necked white woolly jumper over a blue shirt with long collar points, and he explained that the guy playing the guitar who had long brown hair with a Swedish 'porn star' moustache and dressed head to foot in denim was, Norman."

"What was the name of the band?" Hugo asked, interrupting me.

"Hang on, I'm getting to that bit! Anyway, I asked him what the name of his band was, and he would just keep saying that you don't need a fancy name when you're good. I must have asked him about five times what was the name of his band, and he just kept on fobbing me off and repeating you didn't need a fancy name if you're good before I wore him down and he finally told me…"

"Which was, Bert?"

"The Colin and Norman Band! Well, I just couldn't control myself, I just laughed and laughed and laughed, and laughed for the rest of the day," I said laughing out loud.

"That's brilliant, Bert," replied Hugo in fits of laughter also.

"Colin wasn't too pleased though, even now thirty odd years later, whenever I think about it, it just cracks me up."

"I'm not surprised," Hugo replied still laughing along with me.

A Welcome to Leicestershire sign flashed by and then shortly after a sign saying Leicester 13 miles.

"Do you know what the USS Enterprise's captain's name is in the original series of *Star Trek?*"

"Kirk, Bert."

"No, Slog."

"Slog?" Replied Hugo looking puzzled.

"Yeah, at the start of each episode he'd say something like Captain Slog, star date two three one point seven, we are approaching the uninhabited planet Avalon IV to investigate some strange signals."

"Yes, very funny, Bert," said Hugo unamused.

A sign displaying 'For National Space Centre follow M1 (North)' flashed by as we cruised along the M69. "We'll have to visit the Space Centre, Bert, they've got a café, a shop and lots to see."

"Yeah, I haven't been for years, it will make a nice day out, do you and Ruth fancy going out for a carvery on Sunday?"

"Yes, that would be nice, Bert. It's been a while since the last time we had one, where do you fancy going?"

"Gynsells?"

"Yes, I'm looking forward to it already, and Ruth and Julia will enjoy it too," Hugo replied, rubbing his hands together.

"That's what I was thinking. I heard someone on the TV I think, refer to a pint of Guinness as being a roast dinner in a glass."

"Yes, few pints of Guinness down you and you feel like you've eaten a roast dinner."

"Sounds about right, Hugo," I said smiling.

"Oh, you know that woman you pointed out to me, who used to work as a barista at the Costa in Leicester that didn't like coffee?"

"Yeah," I replied.

"Well she's now a bus driver; I saw her the other day driving the number 26."

"I hope she's better at driving a bus than she was as a barista!"

"She can't be any worse, Bert," Hugo replied laughing.

The coach left the motorway and wound its way through Leicester city centre and parked up at St. Margaret's bus station at 17:38. We got up, made sure we had everything and then filed off the coach and collected our bags.

"Let's get a taxi, Hugo."

"You crazy fool, I ain't gettin' in no taxi!" Hugo replied laughing, doing his B. A. Baracus impression as we crossed the road and headed to the taxi rank.

Chapter Twenty-three

As Julia and Ruth both had the day off, Hugo and I had invited them to join us in our Fairy Cake Friday get together at the café in the Beaufort Centre. Julia and I got there early as she had a parcel to post to her sister Louise, who had emigrated with her husband and children to New Zealand many years ago, and I wanted to visit the photo department in the supermarket.

It only took a few minutes to print off a copy of the photo of Hugo holding the cat from my camera, which we encountered before we entered Black Woods, and then I bought a cheap silver coloured frame to put it in.

I looked at my mobile phone, it was 11:50 as I reached the café. "Morning," I said to Hugo and Ruth.

"Morning, Rick."

"Morning, Bert."

"Where's Julia?" Asked Ruth, as I sat down at the table.

"She's just popped to the post office and will be here soon," I replied. Ruth Coldsnow was sat cross legged at the table and according to Hugo was 49 and a widow, she was of medium height, slim, attractive and bubbly, with straight, golden brown fine hair which terminated halfway down her back and had large soft blue eyes. When she giggled she showed her ultra-white but protruding front teeth that could eat an apple through a tennis racquet. Her mauve coloured waterproof jacket was unzipped, revealing a white poplin blouse, which had a neck frill and was worn with black jeans tucked into leopard print ankle boots.

"What the blue blazes are you wearing now?"

"Don't you like it?" Said Hugo, standing up and twirling around to give me the full effect of another gaudy shirt he was wearing.

"Yes, it's err…" I was desperately racking my brains to say something complimentary about it, after I called the shirt he wore on the coach to Wales as belonging to the circus. "It's very colourful Hugo," was all I could manage. Over a plain loose fitting short-sleeved white shirt, it looked as if someone had poured pots of paint in successive stripes, starting from the right shoulder of red, orange, yellow, green, aquamarine and blue, and allowed them to drip down the front, back and sleeves.

"Where do you get these shirts from, eBay?"

"No, Amazon, Bert."

"Aw, I think he looks rather sweet in it," said Ruth with a loving touch of Hugo's arm. "Sweet," I mouthed to Hugo, who grinned at me like a Cheshire cat.

"I'll tell you what I'm waiting on from eBay, DVDs of *Trap Door* and *The Banana Splits*."

"Ooh, you've got to let me borrow them when you've watched them, Bert."

"Don't worry, I will."

"Cheers, Bert."

"Your bracelet must be getting pretty full now, Ruth."

"Yes, it is, Rick, but there's still room for a few more," she said with a smile as she toyed with the teddy bear charm Hugo had bought her in Cardiff. "I always call him my 'teddy bear' don't I hun?"

"You do," answered Hugo coyly.

"And I bet you call him your 'little chu-chi face' in return," I replied as Ruth and Hugo's faces began to redden.

"He also wrote me a lovely verse to go with it."

"Let's hear it then, Hugo?" I teased, winking at Hugo who scrunched up his face and gave out a sigh as he reluctantly began. "I would capture the night stars for you, and fashion them into a necklace, but they would not shine as brightly as your eyes Ruth, so I got you this teddy bear charm instead." Ruth and Hugo sat there gazing into each other eyes, totally enamoured.

"That's beautiful, Hugo," I said smiling to myself.

"I bet you have a pet name for Julia," said Ruth.

"Baby cakes," I said with a smile. "Have you tried your dinosaur flavoured rock yet, Hugo?"

"No, not yet, Bert, have you tried yours?"

"I haven't tried the Fruity Rainbow one yet, but the pasty flavoured one was disgusting, I can't even begin to describe the taste. It didn't taste like any pasty I've ever had before, I only had one bite and had to spit it out and then put the rest of it in the bin!"

"Hmm, doesn't sound good for my dinosaur rock, but what does dinosaur taste like?"

"Chicken," I said, shaking my head.

"I will let you know, Bert."

"Thanks," I replied.

"Watch this, Bert," Hugo said pulling the joke egg he had bought in Barry out of a side pocket of his rucksack.

"Lionel, catch!" Lionel spun around in his chair, a look of horror flashed across his face as the egg left Hugo's hands and spun through the air between Lionel's outstretched hands and landed in his lap. There were a few seconds of deathly silence before Lionel realised he was not covered in egg yolk and with a laugh, threw it back to Hugo who was beside himself with laughter.

"Hi all," said Julia.

"Hi Julia," replied all of us as one, sounding like a chorus.

"Sorry I'm late, but the post office was packed and there was only one man serving, I hope I haven't missed anything."

"No, no," I replied, leaning toward her and giving her a quick kiss on her shimmering, purple coloured lips. Julia wore a short-sleeved black blouse with white spots with a black leather knee-length skirt, black fishnets and black high heels.

"I have just heard a good joke, would you all like to hear it?" Julia asked.

"Yes, we all replied.

"Okay, a parking attendant in a hospital car park tells a man he cannot park in the space he is parking in as it is reserved for badge holders, and the man replies but I do have a bad shoulder!" We all laughed out loud.

"Bad shoulder, I love it," Ruth said, still giggling.

"Anyway, now you are all here, let me show you what I *did* buy from eBay, that came this morning," announced Hugo, unzipping the top of his rucksack and pulling out three hats that he placed on the table. The first one was a black peaked cap with a metal 'Inspector' badge on the front of the black cap band, the second was a red fez with a black tassel, and the third was a dark blue peaked cap with the red 'double arrow' logo of British Rail on the front. I could see where Hugo was going with the inspector's cap and the fez, but I was intrigued by the train cap.

"Very nice, Hugo," I said. With that he picked up the inspector's cap and from the inside pulled out a pre-cut piece of black 'gaffer' tape and placed it on his top lip to simulate a 'toothbrush' moustache, and then put the cap on his head.

"Aw gawd, that's made my day, that has, Butler," he said morphing his face into the self-important Inspector Blake from *On The Buses* before quickly taking off the cap and moustache and replacing it with the fez. He held out his hand, palm down and wiggling his fingers downward. "What's that?" Hugo asked, imitating Tommy Cooper.

"Dunno," I replied, going along with the gag. Hugo reversed his hand, so his fingers were wiggling upwards. "One of those, upside down," he said, bursting into laughter. When Hugo had calmed down, he took off the fez and put on the British Rail cap.

"What do you mean you've lost your Student Rail Card?" He said sternly. By this time, I was in complete fits of laughter as were Hugo, Julia and Ruth. Even Lionel on the next table had a long, slow burning smile spreading across his face which suddenly erupted into a belly laugh, plus the old woman in the corner cracked a smile.

"Well here's another present for you Hugo," I said as I handed over a Forbidden Planet logoed plastic carrier bag, still laughing.

"Cheers Bert," Hugo replied, taking the bag and peering inside. He took out the A4 size, framed photo and held it out in front of him, staring at himself holding the cat we encountered just before entering Black Woods and then passed it to Ruth who smilingly passed it to Julia who also smiled, before passing it back to Hugo. "That's brilliant, thanks, Bert," Hugo said appreciatively.

"I thought you might like it, there's some other bits in there for you," I replied. Hugo rummaged inside the bag and pulled out the *Capricorn One* and *Matinee* DVDs, the 'Cake-o-meter' and another KitKat. "Thanks Bert," Hugo replied with a knowing grin.

I left Hugo reading the blurb on the back covers of the two DVDs as I headed to the café counter to get the coffees and cake, as it was my turn to buy again.

"Four lattes please, and can I have one of these chocolate cakes as well?" I said tapping the glass. The tattoo covered young girl behind the counter removed the cake from the shelf and placed it carefully into a white cardboard box.

"Hurry up Bert, I've got something to tell you!"

"I'm sorry Hugo, you'll have to speak up as I can't hear you over the loud shirt you're wearing."

"Good one, Bert."

"Please tell me you haven't agreed to transport another artefact or something?" I said over my shoulder, dreading the reply.

"No Bert, it's something far more important than that," replied Hugo with excitement in his voice and clutching a letter in his hand.

"Oh right," I replied as I hurriedly paid for the coffees and the cake and returned to the table with two coffees, and then returned to the counter for the other two coffees and then again for the cake and a handful of paper napkins. By this time Hugo looked like he was fit to burst, as I distributed the coffees and placed a handful of sugar sachets and stirrers on the table.

"I'm all ears now, Hugo."

"You know you kept on bugging me to write to Mr Warburton about my Rainbow Bread idea?"

"Yesss."

"Well, I finally got around to doing it just before we went away, and this morning I received a reply."

"Well, don't keep me in suspenders then, Hugo, what does it say, what does it say?" Hugo laughed as he took the letter out of the envelope which had the Warburtons logo on it and unfolded it carefully.

"Dear Mr Twiss," Hugo began. "Thank you for contacting Warburtons and for your suggestion of Rainbow Bread, it is a very interesting concept. I have passed on your idea to our Innovation Team as they are always interested in feedback from our consumers. Yours sincerely, etc., etc." Hugo then passed over the letter to me. I quickly read the headed letter and passed it to Julia, who read it and passed it to Ruth. "I've already read it," said Ruth who then folded it up neatly and passed it back to Hugo. "That's brilliant news Hugo, I'm very pleased for you."

"Well done, Hugo," Julia added.

"Now, you only have to pick a company to pitch your Froot Soop idea to."

"Yes, I will have to do some research first, but I will definitely do it."

"If you go to the soup aisle in any supermarket…"

"Aisle seventeen in Tesco, Bert" Hugo interjected.

"Hmm, and that will give you an idea of the companies that make soup, like Heinz, Baxters. Campbell's etc., that's about the extent of my knowledge of soup makers, but there are dozens more or, you could contact one of the large supermarket chains as they all do their own brand soups."

"I will get on it, but it's not the first soup venture I have had. The first one was 'soup in the basket', but it fell through!" Hugo said laughing at his own joke.

"Old but gold," I said with a smirk.

"Yes but, I have come up with another new idea, Bert, Cheezy with a zed, Feet!"

"What's Cheezy Feet?"

"Basically, it's cheese slices in the shape of a human foot, which I think will appeal to children's sense of fun and the gross, when used on sandwiches or eaten on their own."

"Sounds like another winner, Hugo."

"This time next year, Bert, we'll be millionaires!" Hugo announced, imitating the voice of Del Boy Trotter.

"Let's hope so," I replied, feeling Hugo's infectious optimism.

"I know so, Bert!"

"When I was doing some shopping the other day in the supermarket, I popped across to the jams and spreads aisle to get some marmalade and I noticed they now sell squeezy jam!"

"That's aisle thirty-one."

"You really are a sad person sometimes, Hugo."

"I know, but squeezy jam is the future, Bert."

"Well it's not my future I'm afraid, I will always buy my jam, marmalade, mayo and mustard in a glass jar, and definitely my HP sauce in a glass bottle for as long as possible!"

"Don't turn around, but there's a man on the table in the corner on his phone, and it looks like if he took off his sunglasses, his beard and moustache would come off with them?" Ruth said softly.

Against her advice we all furtively turned around to look at the man. He was chatting on his mobile phone and drinking a cup of coffee. He had a bald head with a black bushy beard and a moustache that started at the top of each ear and wore a pair of designer sunglasses. A plain white T-shirt was stretched tautly across his bodybuilder like physique.

"Yes, it does actually." Hugo said tittering as he turned back around, while Julia and I chuckled to ourselves and Ruth giggled like a chipmunk.

"That's something you could do, Hugo," I said after I had calmed down.

"Yes, I could easily obtain a false beard with a moustache, and I've got a pair of sunglasses I can use, and I can add it to my repertoire," replied Hugo, taking another gulp of his coffee.

"Anyway, Bert, what delights await us in that box?"

"Ah, I thought I would get us something we've never had before," I replied as I opened the box lid. Hugo's eyes grew to the size of saucers as he eyed the chocolate cake with the little piece of flake on the top and was smiling from ear to ear, which reminded me of the shark from *Finding Nemo*.

"The ambassador is spoiling us," Hugo said, rubbing his hands together and leaned down and rooted around inside the bag beside his feet to find the cake-o-meter.

"Shall we begin the ritual, Bert?"

"Ready when you are, Hugo."

"Okay, is it Moody Monday?"

Printed in Great Britain
by Amazon